FLYING THINGS

Michael DiSpezio

Dale Seymour Publications®
Parsippany, New Jersey

Photo Credits
7: Ken Fisher/Stone. 47: U.S. Navy Office of Information East.

Senior Editor: Jeri Hayes
Project Editor: Geri Stewart
Design Manager: Jeff Kelly
Production/Manufacturing Director: Janet Yearian
Production/Manufacturing Manager: Karen Edmonds
Production/Manufacturing Coordinators: Mark Pierce, Lorraine Allen
Cover and Interior Art: Brian Dugan
Section Opener Art: Scott Quick

Dale Seymour Publications
An imprint of Pearson Learning
299 Jefferson Road
Parsippany, NJ 07054
www.pearsonlearning.com
1-800-321-3106

ISBN 1-57232-864-9
1 2 3 4 5 6 7 8 9 10-ML-03 02 01 00

Dale Seymour Publications®

This Book Is Printed On Recycled Paper

A Special Note to Parents and Teachers

Ages ago, kids conquered the classroom sky by flying paper planes. In doing so, they operationally defined paper plane physics. The kids thought they were just having fun. Through innocent and undirected play, they learned the science of flight.

It wasn't long ago that I, too, was flinging gliders across a classroom. It was my physical science class—I was the instructor. Standing in front of thirty adolescents, I was repeating actions that had landed me in detention years before. This time, however, I wasn't disciplined. I was paid.

During my years as a classroom science teacher, I continually searched for things that were fun to do. It didn't matter what the activities were—they just had to be fun. I was confident that science was buried just beneath the surface; all I had to do was scrape off the sugar coating and I'd uncover another vehicle for teaching science.

Flying Things is packed with those vehicles. As you'll discover, ***Flying Things*** isn't just a book—it's a complete and friendly learning experience. Written in language kids understand, it is an ideal adventure in self-paced fun. In other words, "No Adult Required!"

The concepts embedded in this book are presented in a sound (but not absolute) sequence. Any kid working through the activities in the book from beginning to end will experience (but perhaps never realize) an increasing conceptual development. By the end of the book, he or she will have constructed an understanding of what keeps things flying.

In the classroom, this book can support an independent module on flight. If, however, a large block of time is impractical, individual activities can enrich your current curriculum. As you'll discover, the content gracefully enhances classroom topics such as transportation, technology, birds, and the atmosphere. In addition to conceptual delivery, most projects can easily be tweaked into arenas for critical and creative thinking.

Flying Things can be used as a random access treasury. It is a library of quick, fun, and motivating learning experiences. Kids can jump from one project to another, filling rainy afternoons or extra periods. However, if they do tackle the activities out of order, they may need to flip back to earlier activities to get a better understanding of concepts they skipped over. The activities can even spark ideas for science fair projects or become the focus of school competitions.

Instead of reading about this adventure, why not experience it right now? As a parent or teacher, you earned your takeoff clearance long ago. Just fire up that cerebral engine—***the sky's the limit!***

Contents

Materials List

The Protoprop
- Paper plate
- Scissors
- Cotton-tipped swab
- White glue or hot glue gun

The Papercopter
- Blackline Master pattern
- Paper clip
- Scissors

The Flutter Faller
- Blackline Master pattern
- Scissors

The Circling Cylinder
- Blackline Master pattern
- Scissors
- Tape

The Sassy Saucer
- Five paper plates
- Tape
- Scissors

The Flying Wing
- Blackline Master pattern
- Scissors

The Osprey
- Blackline Master pattern
- Scissors

The T-Wing
- Blackline Master pattern
- Scissors

The Delta-1
- Blackline Master pattern
- Scissors
- Tape

The Tray Bien
- Plastic foam meat tray
- Scissors
- Paper clips
- Tape

The Straw de Loop
- Blackline Master pattern
- Straw
- Tape
- Scissors

The Flying Napkin
- Blackline Master pattern
- Tape

The Boomerang
- Blackline Master pattern
- Cardboard stock (cereal or clothes box sides)
- Scissors
- Paste

The Parachute
- Blackline Master pattern
- Thread (or kite string)
- Plastic garbage bag
- Centimeter ruler
- Scissors
- Tape
- Small toy (cargo)
- Paper clip

The Paraglide
- Blackline Master pattern
- Thread (or kite string)
- Plastic garbage bag
- Five straws
- Scissors
- Tape
- Paper clips (several large ones)

The Balloon Rocket
- Balloon
- Straw
- Kite string
- Scissors
- Tape

The Dragonfly
- Blackline Master pattern
- Two straws
- Scissors
- Tape
- Index card
- Clay

The Rocket-Powered Dragonfly
- Basic Dragonfly glider
- Balloon
- Straw
- Small rubber band
- Tape

Prepare for Takeoff

Fasten your seat belts. You are about to take off on a fantastic journey into the world of flying things. As you've probably guessed, this isn't a plain old book. It's a hands-on adventure where you get to build, create, and fly all sorts of flying things. You'll also learn about the science and history of flight, not just by reading but by doing things. Ready to start? ***Great!***

Let the countdown begin:

5 . . . 4 . . . 3 . . . 2 . . . 1.

Whirling
Wonders

The Protoprop

Before there were airplanes, there were propellers. In fact, this flying thing is based upon an antique propeller toy. Carved in the shape of a propeller, this wooden flyer was launched skyward by kids who had no concept of electronic recreations.

Materials

- paper plate
- scissors
- cotton-tipped swab
- white glue (and patience) or hot glue gun and CAUTION!

To Build:

1. Carefully twist off the cotton from both ends of a cotton-tipped swab.
2. Trace this pattern onto a paper plate.

3. Use your scissors to carefully cut out the pattern.
4. Mark the center of this "blade" with an *X*.
5. Have an adult place a spot of hot glue on the *X*. Carefully position one end of the swab on the hot glue. Hold the pieces steady until the glue hardens.

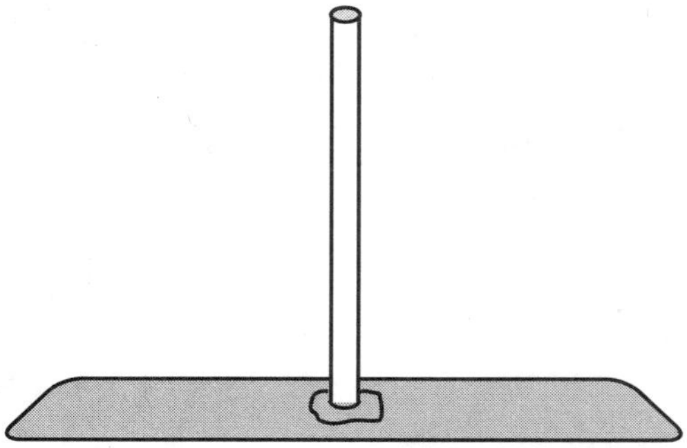

6. Turn over your contraption. Congratulations! You have built your first flying machine—the ***Protoprop***.

Now, you're ready for the test launch.

Basic (but stable) Fall Experiment

1. **Wear eye protection.**
2. Place the Protoprop shaft between your two hands.
3. Quickly slide your palms across each other. As your hands move, the Protoprop will spin.
4. When your hands separate, the Protoprop continues to whirl and falls gently to the ground.

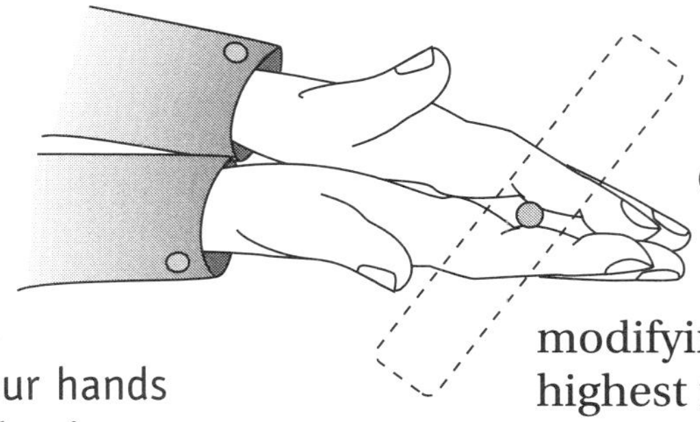

Change the angle of the bend. How does this affect the Protoprop's flying ability? Keep modifying the blades until you've built the highest flying contraption. Good luck.

(See ***Flying Facts:*** *Right-handed and Left-handed Props* on page 4 for the answer.)

Taking Off

Now that you've observed the protoprop in a stable fall, let's modify it into a flying machine that goes up.

1. Carefully put a slight downward "twist" in each of the two propeller blades. The two bends should be placed on opposite sides of the prop as shown here.

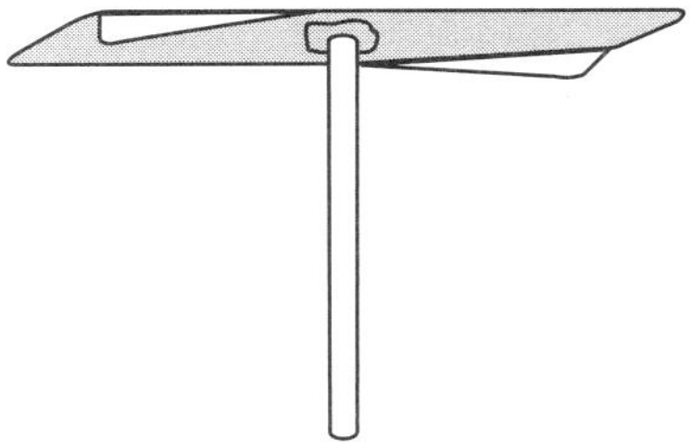

2. Try your launch again. When you slide your palms, make sure that the downward edge of each blade leads the spinning direction. What happens if you reverse the direction of the spin? Make a guess. Then, try it to find out!

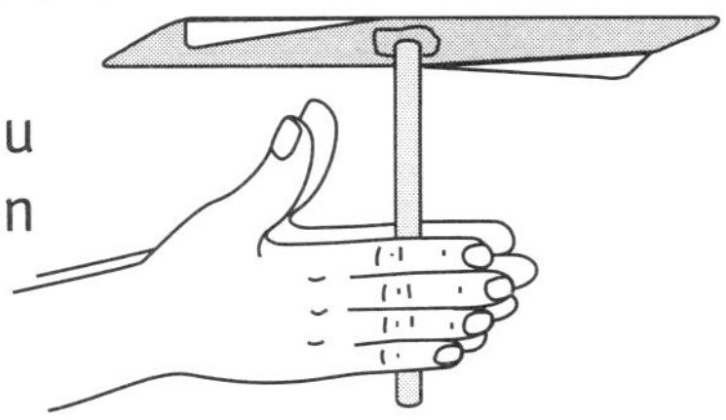

Flying Facts

The Air Screw

Did you know that a propeller is also known as an air screw? Take a good look at a propeller and you can see its resemblance to a hardware screw. As the propeller spins, its slanted blades twist into the air. This twisting motion cuts into the air ahead of the prop. Like a turning metal screw, the propeller advances ahead carrying anything attached, such as the body of the plane with passengers and crew, forward.

Flying Facts

Prop Pitch

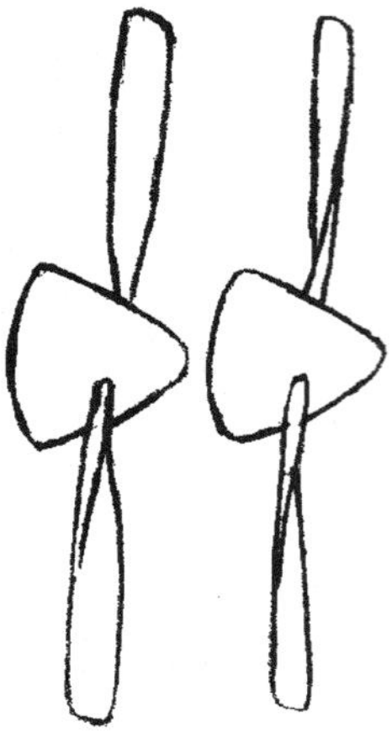

Unlike the Protoprop blades, the blades of most aircraft propellers are not fixed in one position. While they are spinning, the angle at which the blades strike the air can be changed. This angle, known as the *pitch* of the prop, controls how much force the spinning propeller produces. By changing the pitch, the pilot can vary the "bite" of the spinning blades.

Lift and Weight

The Protoprop works like a helicopter. The spinning propeller blades create an upward force. This upward force is called *lift.* Lift counteracts the craft's downward force, or *weight.* When the lift is greater than the weight, the Protoprop rises. When the weight is greater, the Protoprop descends.

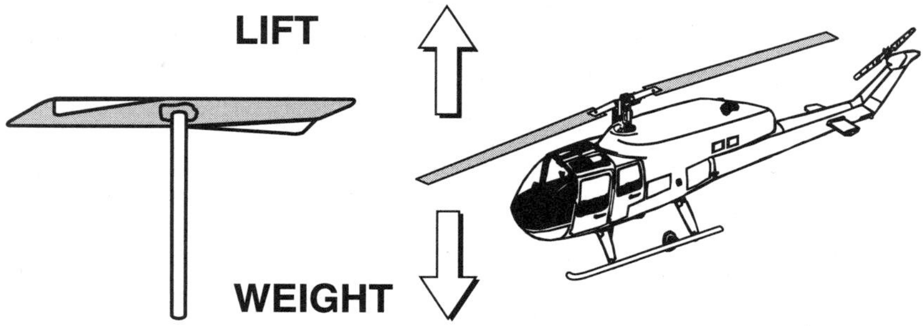

Right-Handed and Left-Handed Props

Have you ever tried to tighten a screw by turning the screw counterclockwise? If so, you quickly realized that it can't be done. The threads of a screw are positioned so that the screw moves into the wood only when turned clockwise. The screw pulls out of the wood when it is turned counterclockwise.

The blades of a flying craft's propeller, like the threads of a screw, determine which way the craft travels. Spin your Protoprop one way, and the force is directed upward. Spin it in the opposite direction, and the force no longer lifts the prop but stabilizes its descent. This stability comes from the spinning motion—not the lift.

The Papercopter

Have you ever heard the old saying "What goes up, must come down"? If so, what do you think it means?

There are many different ways things can come down. This next flying thing produces a lively, spinning motion. It's called a Papercopter.

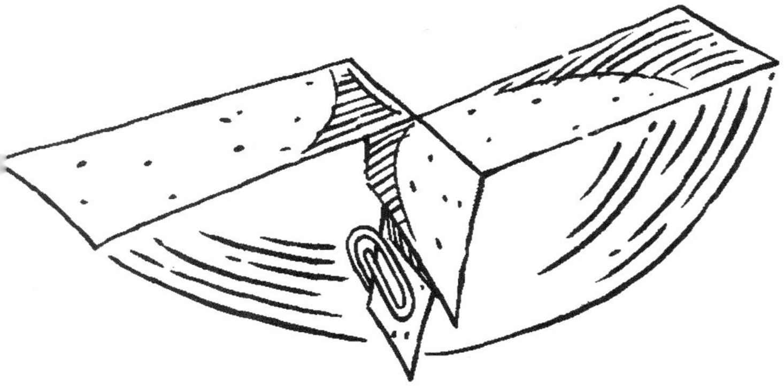

Materials

- Papercopter Blackline Master, page 53
- paper clip
- scissors

To Build:

1. Turn to the Plane Patterns section at the back of this book. Photocopy the **Papercopter** pattern on page 53.

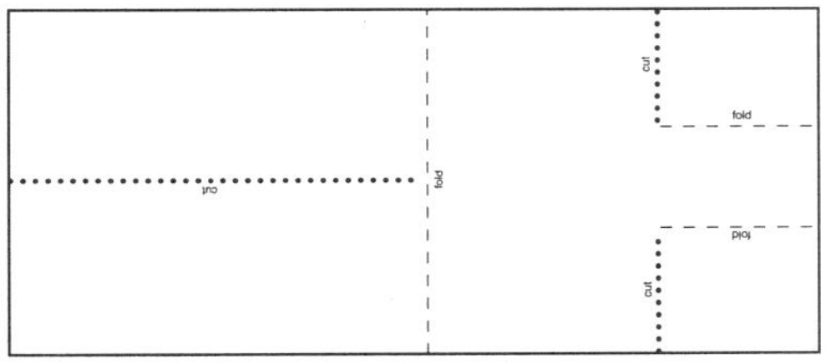

2. Use scissors to cut out the pattern. Then cut along the dotted lines. One cut will separate the two wings. The other two cuts will help form the stabilizing bottom folds.

3. Fold each bottom section over along the dashed lines. Secure with a paper clip.

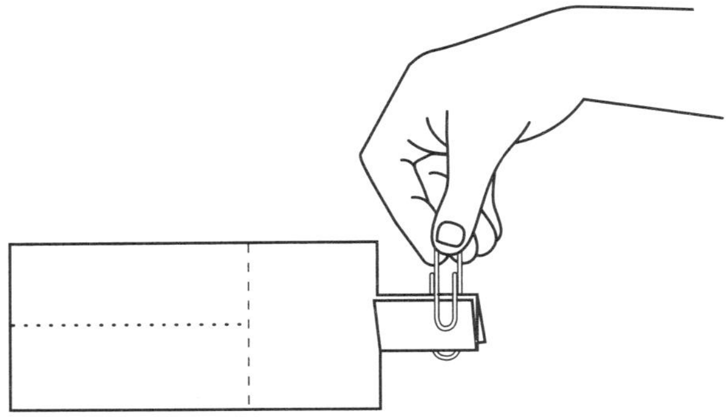

4. Fold one wing in one direction. Fold the other wing in the opposite direction.

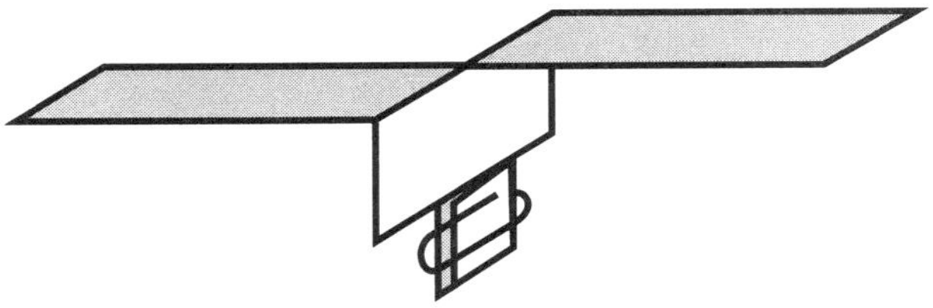

The Test Flight

1. Hold the Papercopter by the tips of both wings.

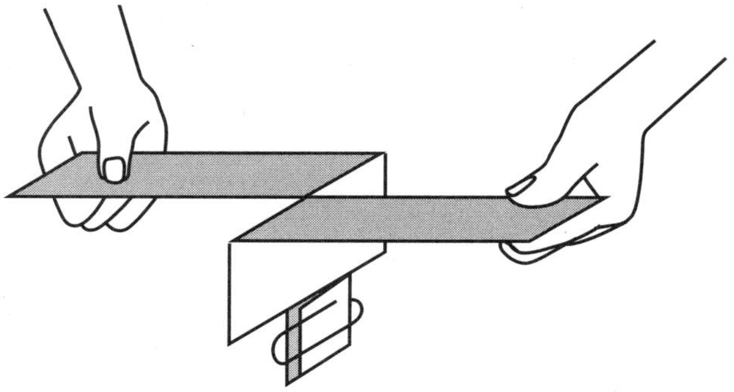

2. Release the Papercopter.

Flying Facts

Helicopter Seeds

The seeds of sycamore trees spin like a Papercopter. Light winds can carry these flying seeds. This adaptation helps spread out the new sycamore plants. By landing far away from where it was launched, the young sycamore doesn't have to compete for sunlight with its parent. If you can find a sycamore seed, try to guess which way the seed will spin. Test your guess.

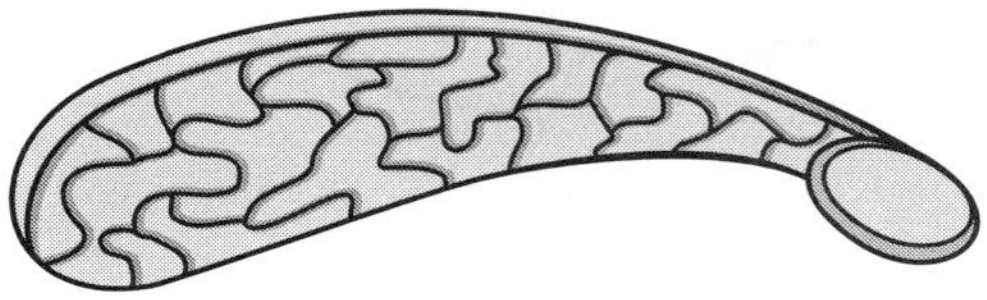

Taking Off

1. Did your Papercopter spin clockwise or counterclockwise (from looking down)?
2. Repeat the drop three more times.
3. From what you observed, do you think the spin direction is random? If not, how can you change the Papercopter design so that it spins in the opposite direction?

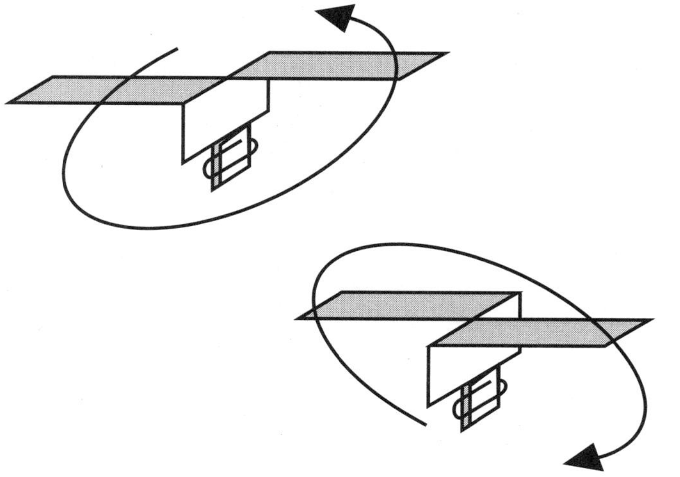

One Step Further

Become an engineer! Design a Papercopter that has a slower spin. You can change as many things about its design as you'd like.

Flying Facts

Free Falling

Did you know that sky divers can control the rate of speed at which their bodies fall? By changing the way their bodies encounter the air, they can slow down or increase the rate of fall. If there was no air, the fall would continue to accelerate. Because there is air, the falling speed has a limit. The "free fall" speed limit is set by the collisions the body makes with the surrounding air particles. No matter how sky divers twist or distort their bodies, the fall can't be faster than the limit set by air resistance.

The Flutter Faller

When a pitcher throws a baseball, he or she makes sure that the ball has a spin. Not only does the spinning motion produce hard-to-hit curves, sinkers, and risers, but it also creates the stability needed for the pitch to stay on target.

The next flying thing is called a flutter faller. Like a baseball, spinning gives it stability.

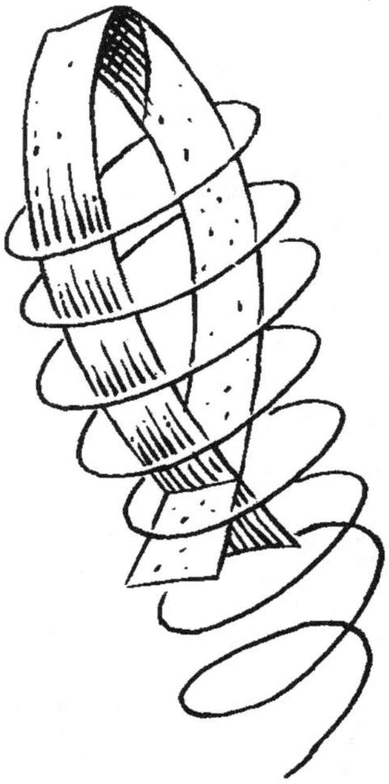

Materials

- **Flutter Faller Blackline Master, page 55**
- **scissors**

To Build:

1. Turn to the Plane Patterns section at the back of this book. Photocopy the **Flutter Faller** pattern on page 55.

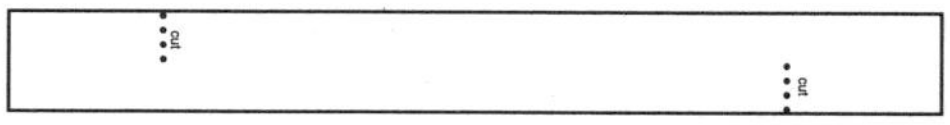

2. Cut out the Flutter Faller pattern. Make two cuts along the dotted lines.

3. Curl the strip into a loop.

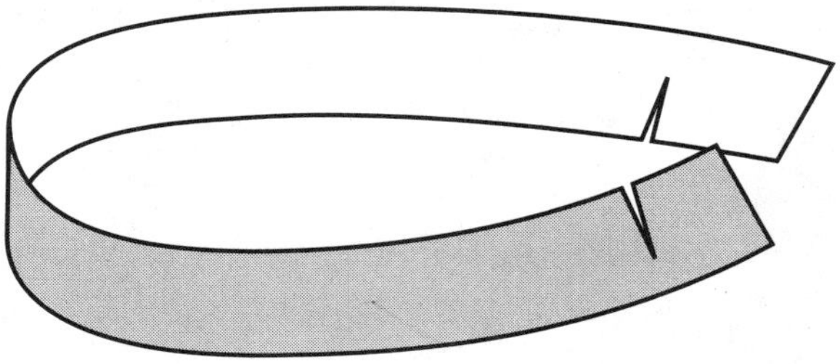

4. Insert one notch into the other.

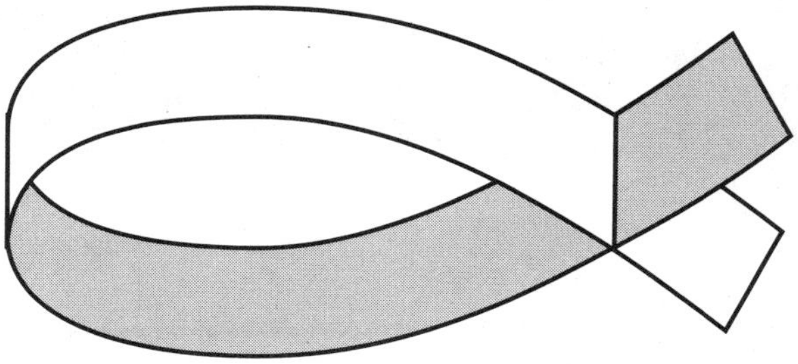

Test Flight

Release the Flutter Faller and watch it flutter through the air! You'll get the best flutter if you release the Flutter Faller in a sideways position. You can also get a good flutter by pulling your hand out from under it (as if pulling a carpet out from under it). If you release the Flutter Faller head down or tail down, it may not have enough time to rotate into a sideways position and develop the fluttering spin.

Double Flutter

Here's a flutter pattern that can be used to construct a double-loop flutter! Build it and compare it with the single-loop version.

Taking Off

The Flutter Fallers, like the Papercopter, can spin in either a clockwise or counterclockwise direction. Can you alter the design so that it falls with the opposite spin? If so, how?

Can you design a pattern that can be used to build a triple-loop flutter?

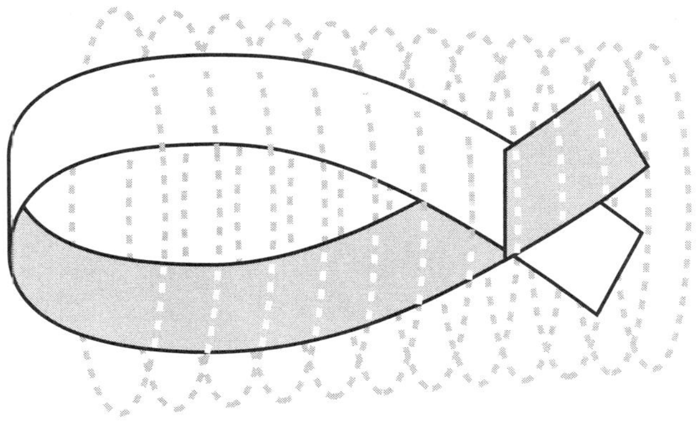

The Circling Cylinder

Ever spin a top? If so, you know that a spinning top stays balanced. The faster the top spins, the more stable the top remains. When the top slows, it loses stability and falls over.

The Flutter Fallers that you built in the previous activity also gained stability by spinning. When they didn't spin, they drifted along an unpredictable path. When they spun, however, they became more stable.

The next flying thing is called a Circling Cylinder. It should be launched like a football. Otherwise, its cylindrical shape can easily cause it to tumble out of control.

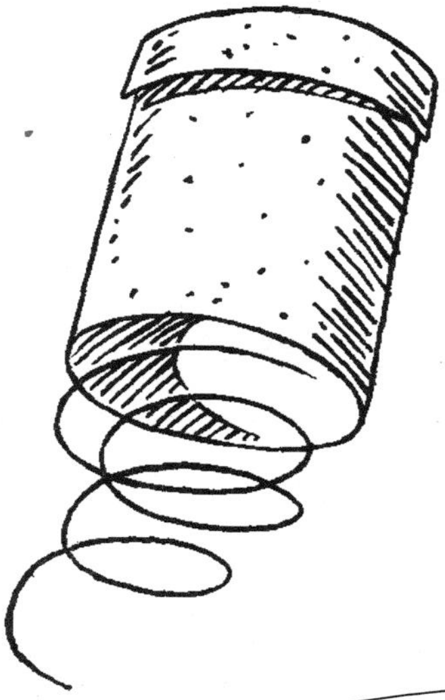

Materials

- **Circling Cylinder Blackline Master, page 57**
- **scissors**
- **tape**

To Build:

1. Turn to the Plane Patterns section at the back of this book. Photocopy the **Circling Cylinder** pattern on page 57.

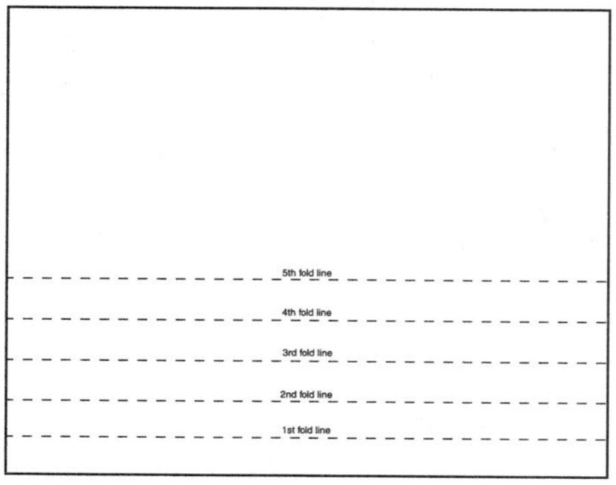

2. Use scissors to cut out the Circling Cylinder pattern.
3. Fold back and crease the leading edge of the glider pattern along the first fold line.

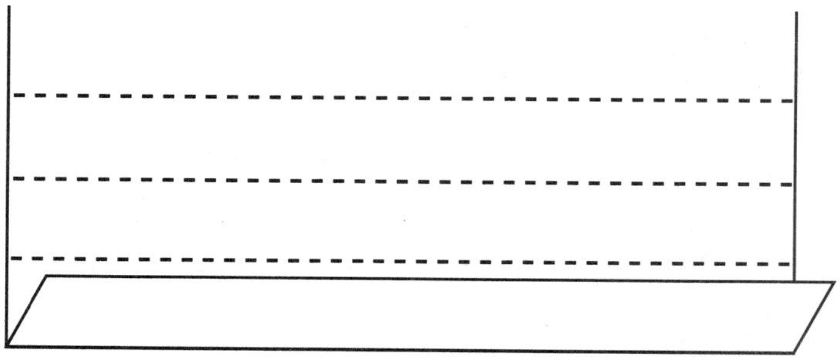

4. Then, fold the next edge (marked with a "2") back and crease. The folds should be made in the same direction. In other words, do not make an accordion-style fold.

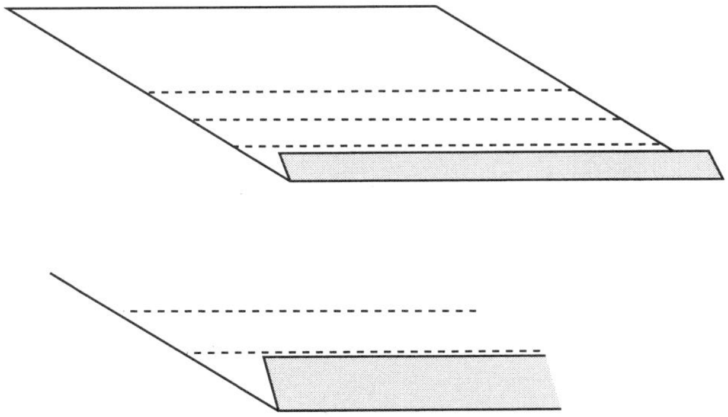

5. Continue folding until you fold the last line.

6. Coil the pattern into a cylinder.

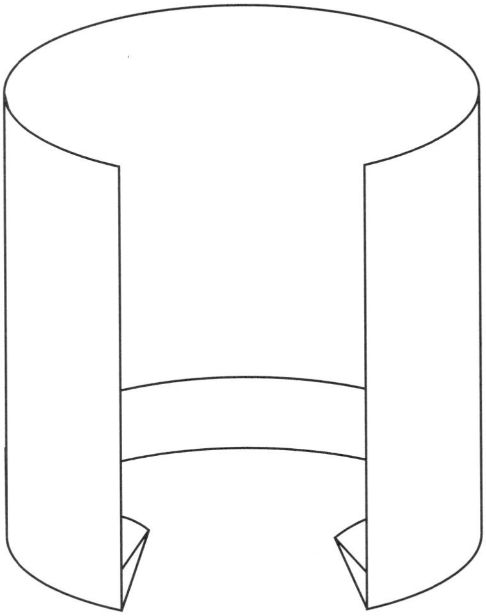

7. To secure, interweave the folds of the leading edge. Secure it with a section of tape.

Launching

Hold the cylinder in your hand and throw it so that the folded leading edge is in front. As it leaves your hand, place a gentle spin on the craft as if it were a football.

The Sassy Saucer

Have you ever seen a flying saucer? How about a flying cup? Maybe a soaring spoon? Perhaps a floating fork?

Well, here's your chance to build a Sassy Saucer. This basic design will get you started. Once you've constructed this one, you may want to build and decorate a model that looks like an actual alien spacecraft.

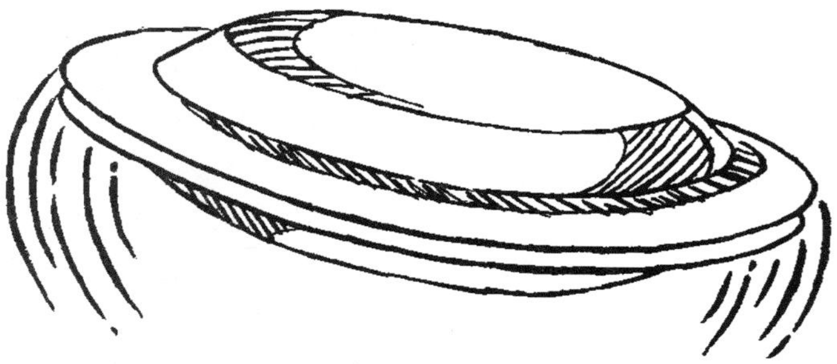

Materials

- five paper plates
- tape
- scissors

To Build:

1. Gather five paper plates, tape, and scissors to build the Sassy Saucer.
2. Use scissors to carefully remove the round, flat bottom of five paper plates. Do not cut through the plate rims.

3. Stack four of the plate rims. Use tape to wrap them together in four equally spaced places around the rim. These plates form the bottom half of the saucer.

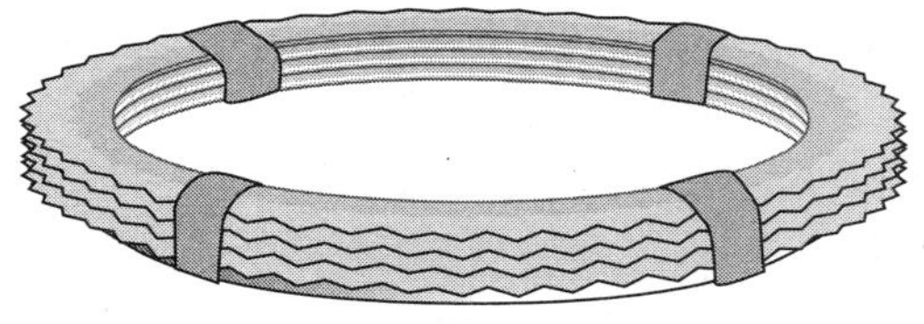

4. Place the other plate rim onto this stack so that the upper rims touch. Secure the upper and lower saucer halves together with eight pieces of tape evenly spaced.

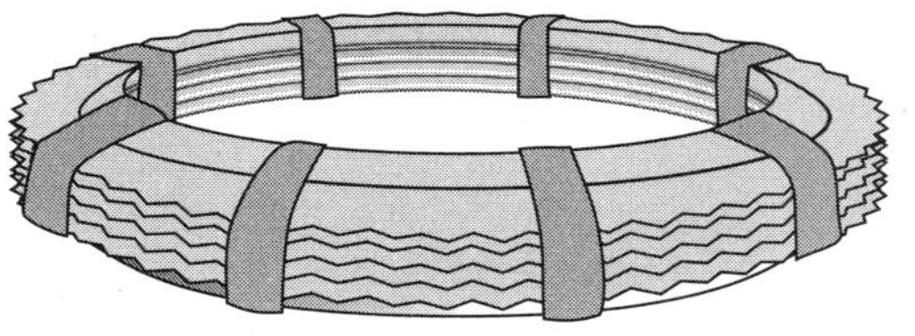

Test Flight

To fly this saucer, hold it and bend your wrist in. Release your wrist with a throwing motion and the craft should spin quite a distance!

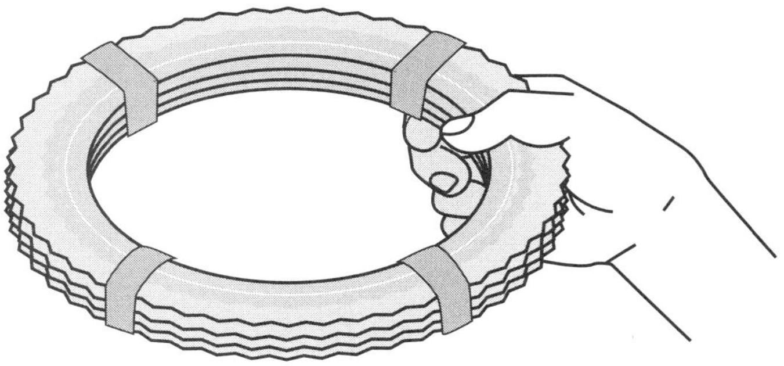

Taking Off

Does your saucer have a tendency to tip in one direction? If so, try throwing it with your other hand. What happens when the saucer spins in the opposite direction?

Take off the upper rim and turn it upside down. Use tape to secure the rim in its new upside-down position. Does this change alter the flying characteristics of the saucer?

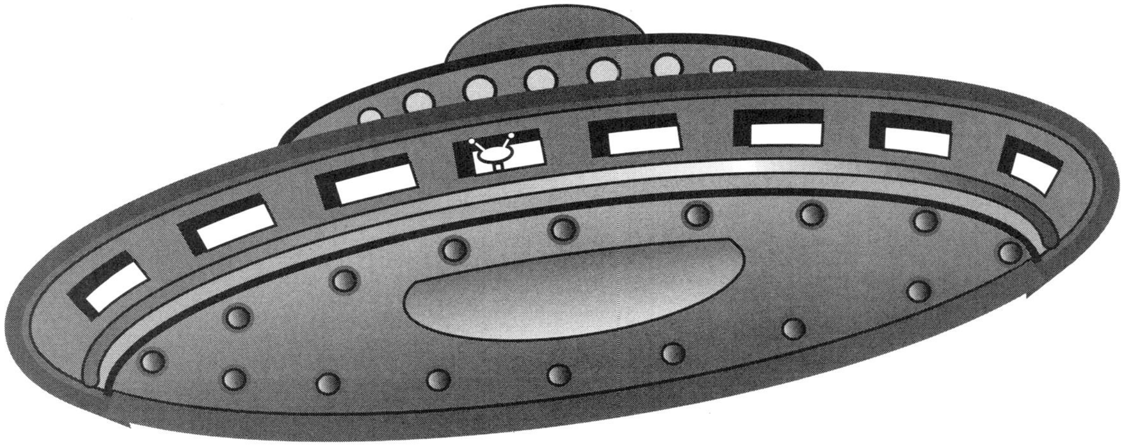

Things with Wings

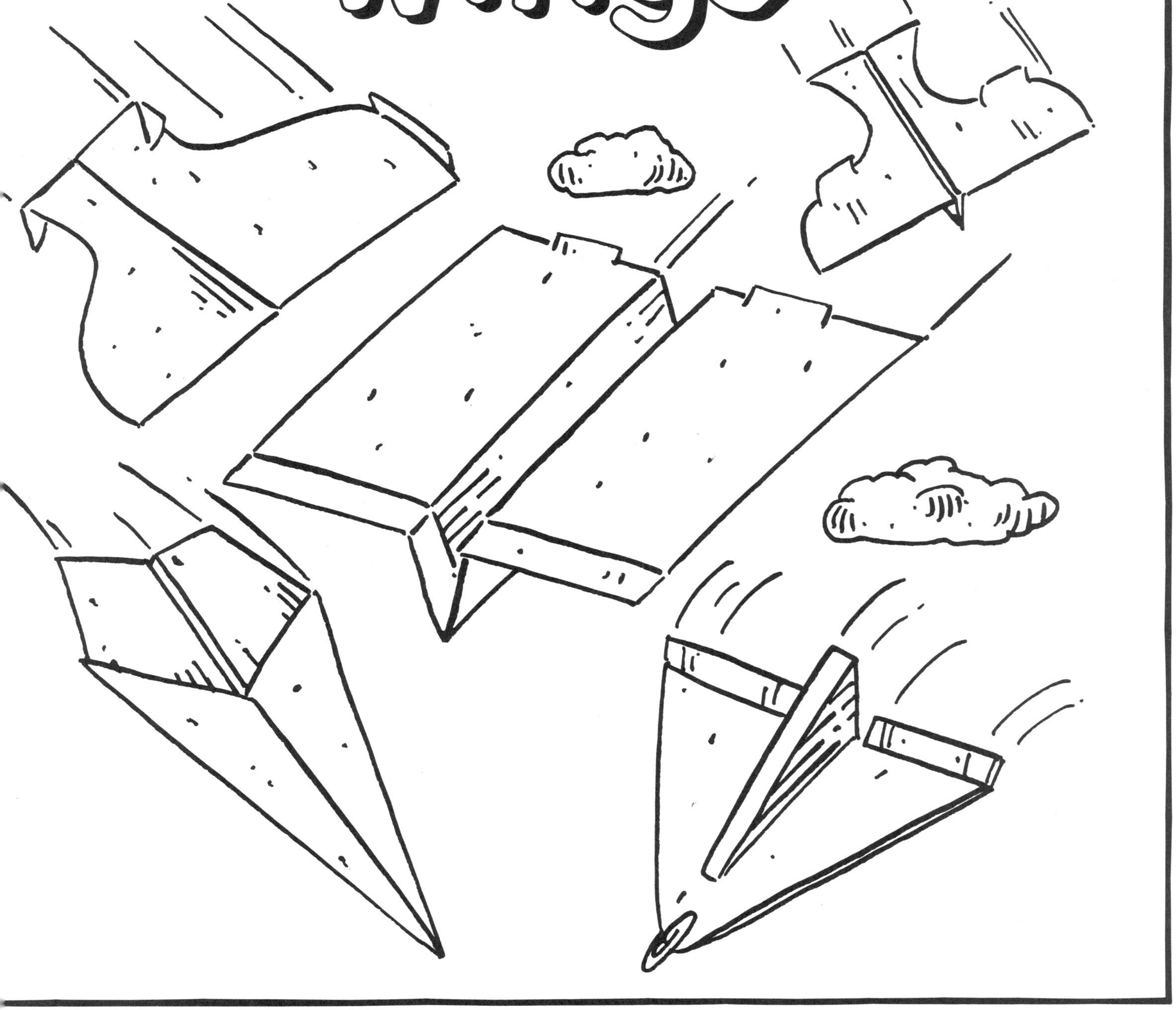

The Flying Wing

The Flying Wing is an ideal model to investigate the forces that keep things flying. *Weight* is the downward force that makes things descend. *Lift* is the upward force that counteracts weight.

Everything in the air takes part in a balancing act between lift and weight. If the lift is greater than the weight, the object goes up. If the weight is greater, the craft descends. What do you think happens if the lift and weight are equal?

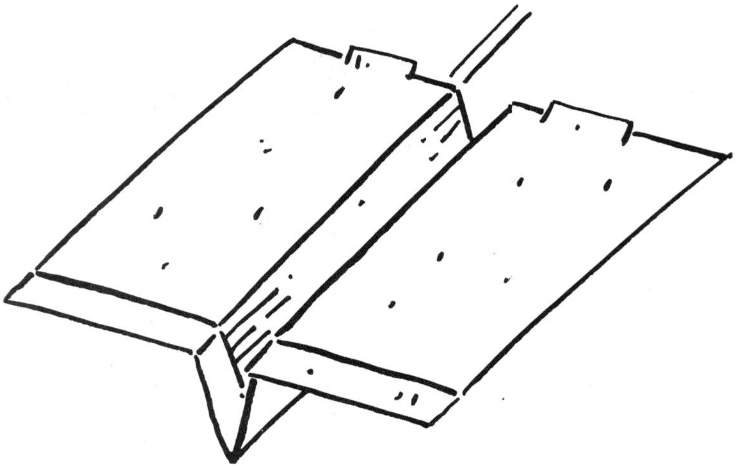

To Build:

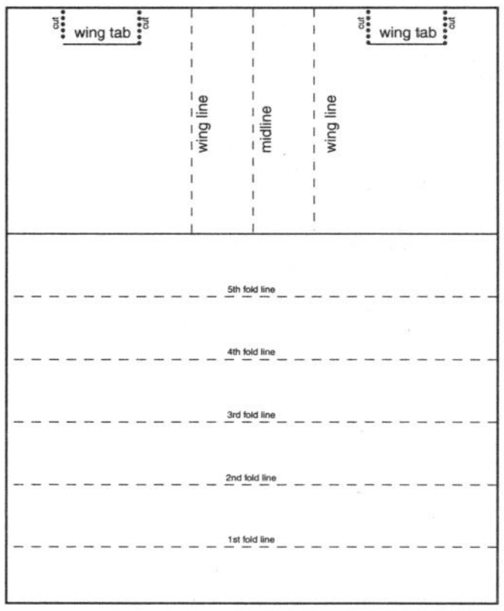

1. Turn to the Plane Patterns section at the back of this book. Photocopy the **Flying Wing** pattern on page 59.
2. Fold back along the first fold line.
3. Then, fold along the second fold line so that it wraps around the first fold. Continue folding until all the dashed lines have been creased and folded back.

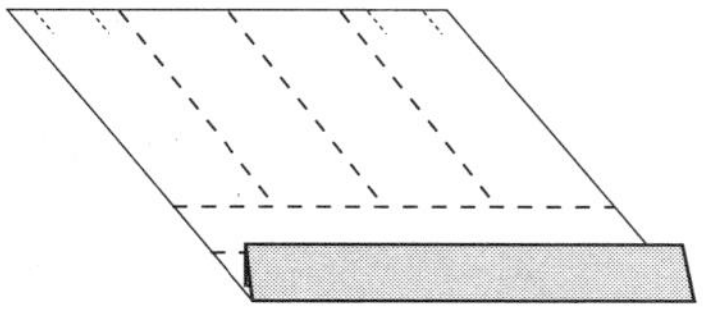

4. Fold the whole body along its midline, as shown here.

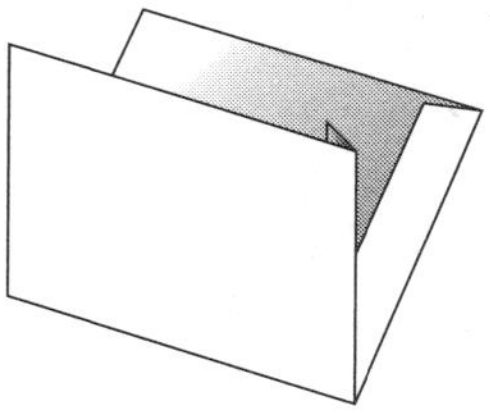

5. Bend down each wing along the dotted wing lines. Presto! It's done.

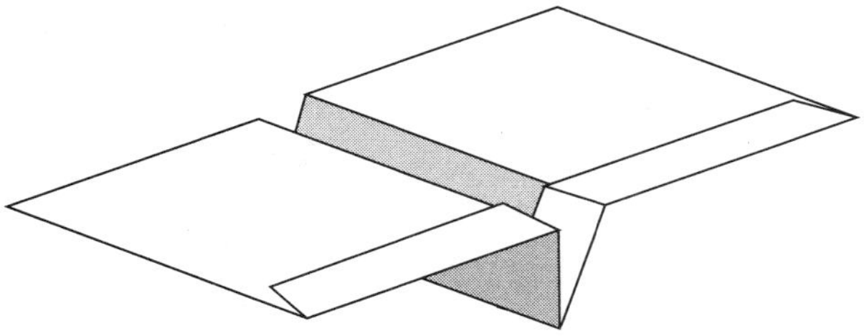

Materials

- Flying Wing Blackline Master, page 59
- scissors

Test Flight

1. Hold the Flying Wing in the middle of its bottom double-folded edge. With a very gentle throw, release the glider.
2. If the Flying Wing dives, there is not enough lift. To produce more lift, unfold the leading edge by one crease.
3. If the Flying Wing stalls, there is too much lift. To produce less lift, fold and crease the leading edge one more time. (See ***Flying Facts:*** *Too Much of a Good Thing*, page 18.)
4. When you reach the right balance between lift and weight, the Flying Wing will glide effortlessly across the room.

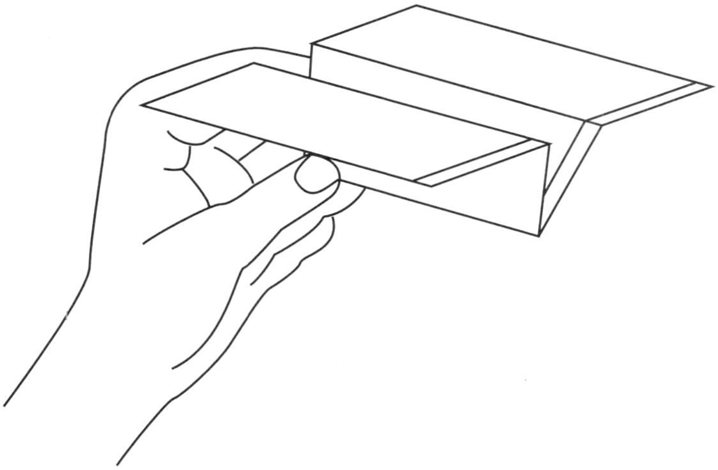

Flying Facts

The Flying Wing Bomber

Decades ago, the U.S. Air Force tried to develop a flying wing bomber. Due to instability, however, this craft never made it beyond the experimental stage. It wasn't until the development of specialized computers that flying wings made a comeback. These "electronic pilots" continually monitor a craft's balance and position. This data is then used to automatically correct the craft's flight path. Modern military craft such as the B-2 Stealth bomber are based on the flying wing design.

Flying Facts

Too Much of a Good Thing

The wings of an aircraft create lift. Without wings, planes couldn't stay in the air. Having too much lift can also be a problem! If the lift is too strong, the plane climbs steeply. If it climbs too steeply, it looses lift and stalls. When a craft stalls, it wobbles out of control and falls to the ground.

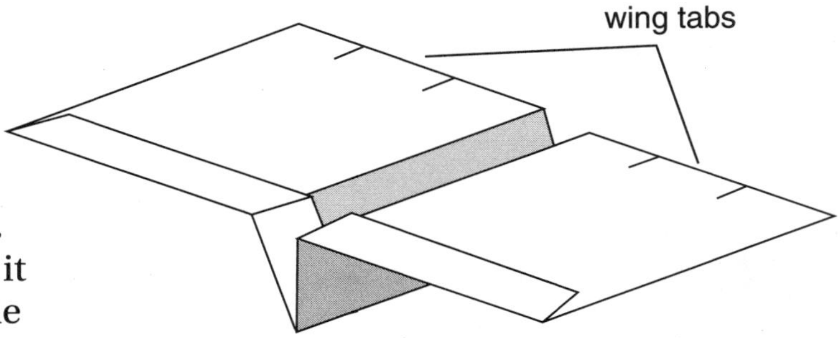

Wing Tabs

***The Flying Wing's flight path can be controlled by small folds called* wing tabs.** When the tab is bent away from the wing, it extends into the passing air. Air striking the tab exerts a tiny push. That push changes the path of the craft.

Use scissors to make a wing tab in the trailing edge of both wings of your Flying Wing model. If the plane dives, bend the tabs up. If the plane stalls, bend the tabs down. What do you think would happen if you bent one tab up and the other tab down? After you have made your guess, try it to find out!

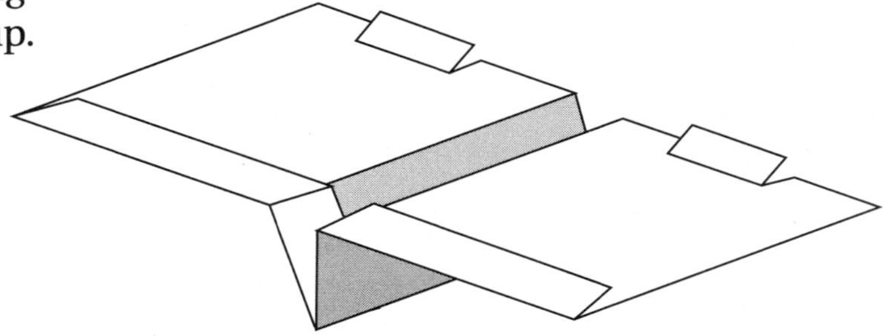

The Osprey

Unlike the Flying Wing, the Osprey you will make in this activity has a cut-out body. The body of an aircraft is called a *fuselage*.

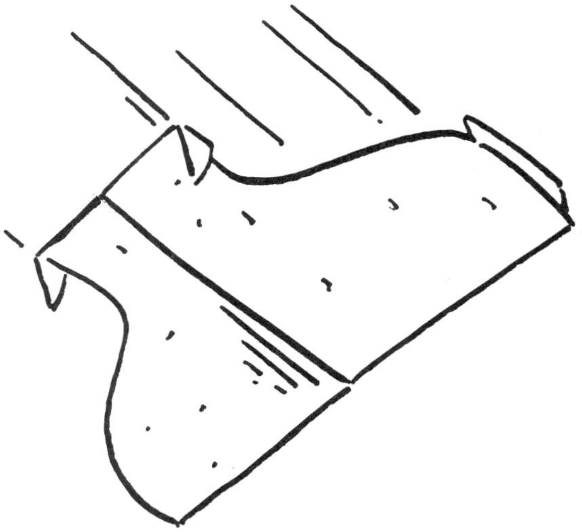

This Osprey is based on a design by Ralph Barnaby, an aviator who soared high above the clouds in hot air balloons. During his trips, he'd build and release paper gliders. From his high perch, he'd watch his gliders circle below.

Stabilizer

In addition to the large wing, the Osprey has a smaller winglike part at the tail. This section is called a *horizontal stabilizer* or *stabilizer* for short. As its name suggests, it adds stability to the Osprey by keeping its tail section level.

Winglets

To add more stability, the tips of the Osprey's wings and stabilizer are bent. These bends are called *winglets*. The tips on the wing section are bent upward. The tips on the stabilizer are bent downward. Many modern aircraft also have winglets.

Materials

- **Osprey Blackline Master, page 61**
- **scissors**

To Build:

1. Turn to the Plane Patterns section at the back of this book. Photocopy the **Osprey** pattern on page 61.

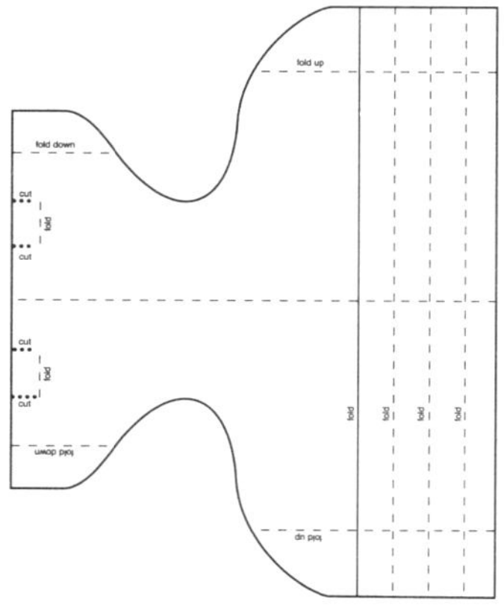

2. Use scissors to carefully cut out the outline of the Osprey.
3. Fold back to make a leading edge.

❹ Continue folding back this edge in a spiral wrap until the folds reach the solid line.

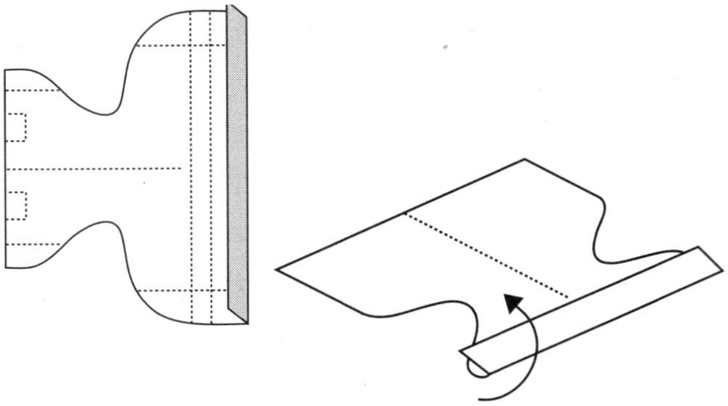

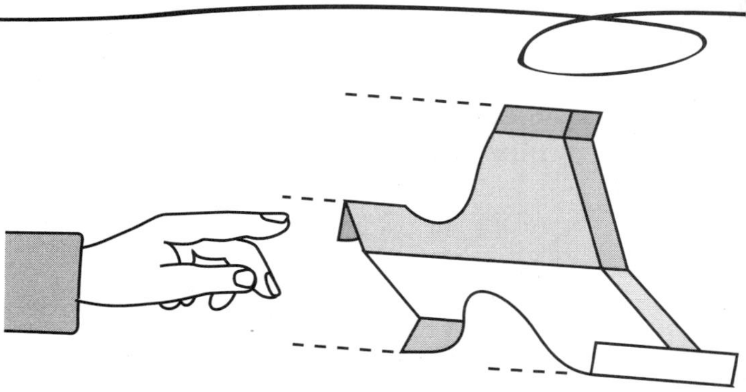

An unstable Osprey flight is easily corrected. If it dives, you need more lift. Unfold a crease from the leading edge to create more wing area and more lift. If it stalls, you need less lift. Fold up one more crease on the leading edge to decrease the wing area and reduce the lift.

❺ Fold the glider in half lengthwise along the midline. Then, bend the sides back down so that the wings form a slight angle along the crease.

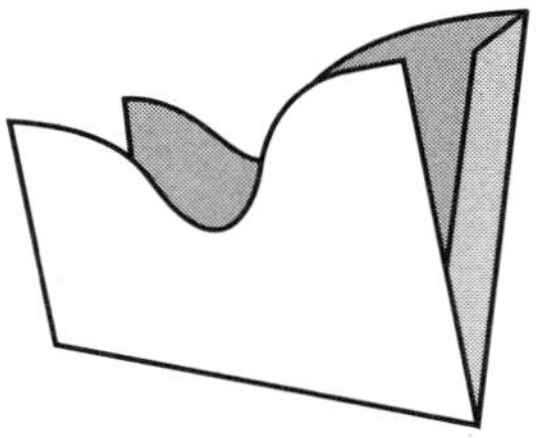

❻ Fold down the two stabilizer winglets.

❼ Fold up the two wing winglets.

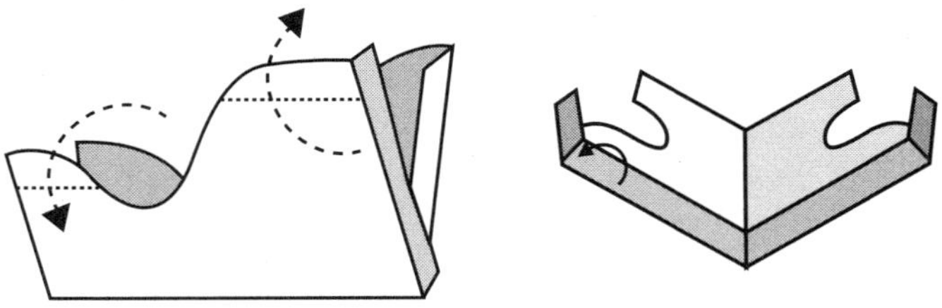

Flying the Osprey

To fly the Osprey, hold the glider on the middle of its bottom edge. Gently throw the Osprey forward.

Elevators

To help steer this glider, you can add steering tabs. These and other tabs that control the flight path are called *control surfaces*. The control surface found on the stabilizer is an *elevator*. Elevators control the up/down position of the craft's front end. By the way, this front end of the fuselage is called the *nose*.

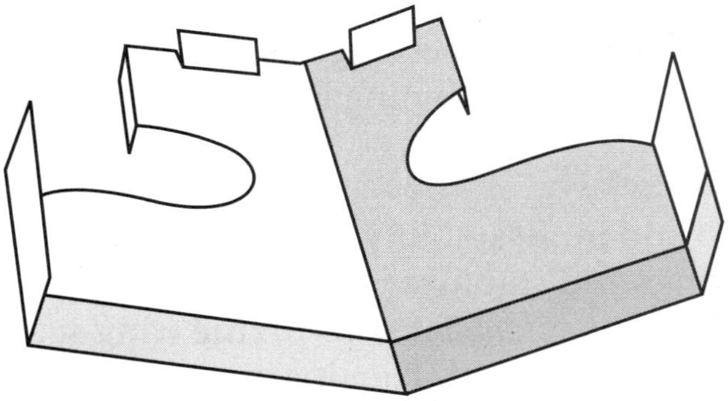

Elevators bent upward cause the nose of the glider to rise. In contrast, elevators bent downward cause the nose to go down.

The T-Wing

The T-Wing is another glider that has a cutout fuselage section. Its slick design and control surfaces make it great for stunt flying.

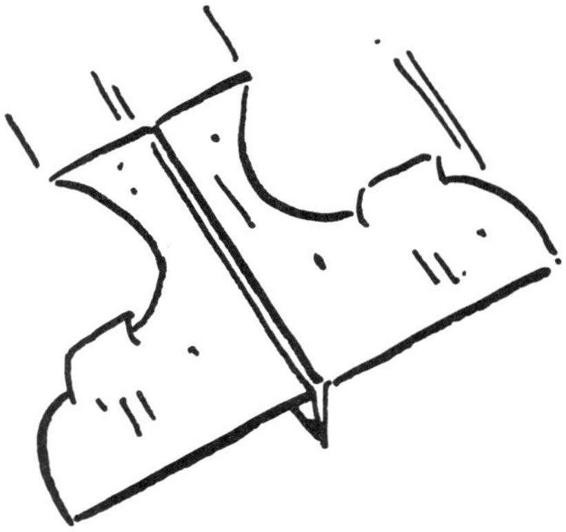

Materials

- T-Wing Blackline Master, page 63
- scissors

To Build:

❶ Turn to the Plane Patterns section at the back of this book. Photocopy the **T-Wing** pattern on page 63.

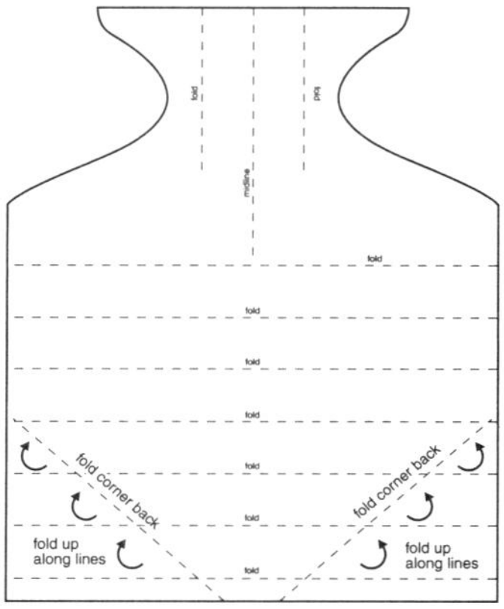

❷ Cut out the model. Make sure to trim the tail of the glider carefully.

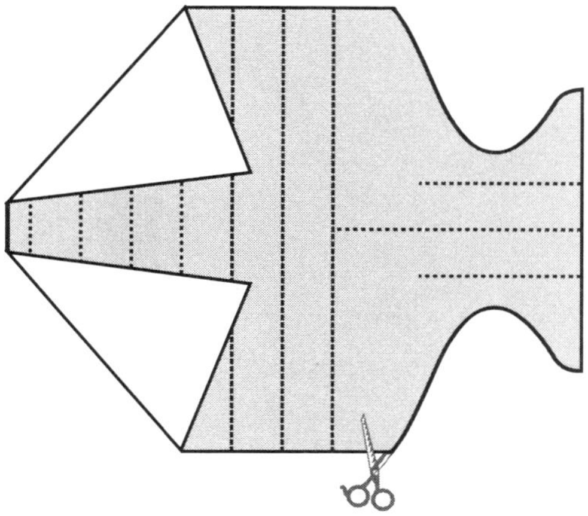

❸ Fold up the leading corners to form an angular nose.

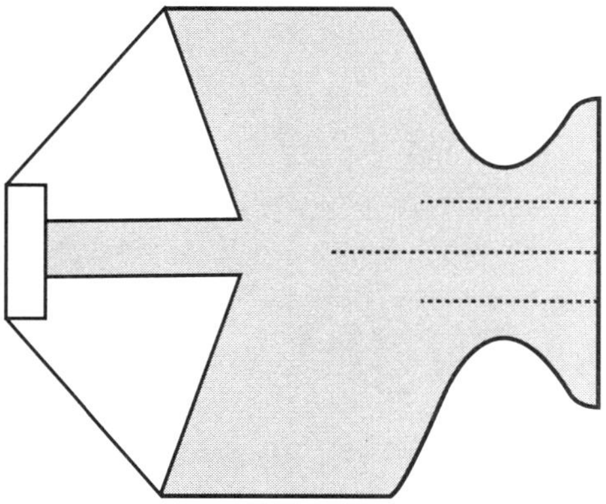

❹ Fold up the nose along the dashed lines.

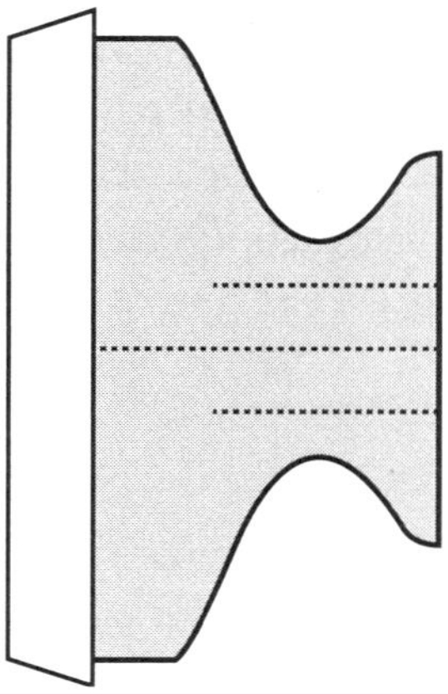

5. Fold the plane in half lengthwise along the midline.

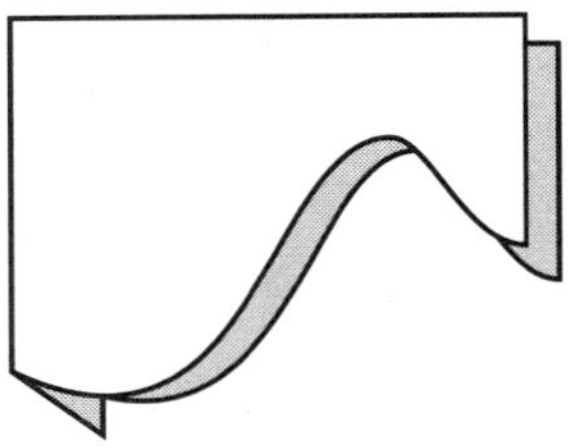

6. Fold out both sides of the plane along the lines marked *fuselage*.

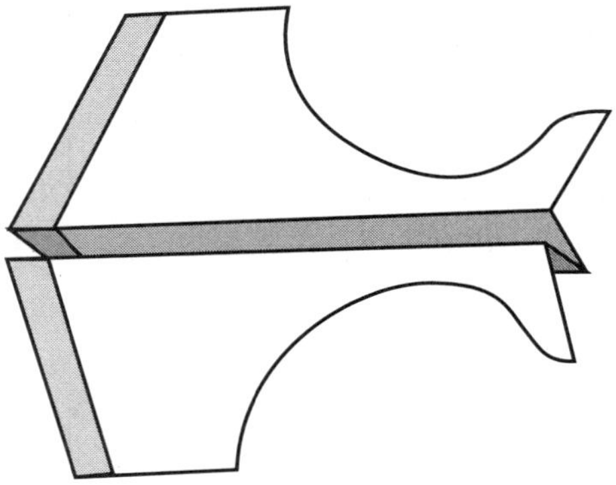

Test Flight

Throw your T-Wing and watch it fly! Then, customize your T-Wing by adding rudders and ailerons.

The tail section of this commercial jet has two stabilizing surfaces. The sideways surface is called the *horizontal stabilizer* or just plain *stabilizer*. The control surfaces of the stabilizer are called *elevators*.

The up-and-down surface is called the *vertical stabilizer* or *fin*. The fin keeps the tail from sloshing back and forth. The control surface on the fin is called the *rudder*.

The tail of the T-Wing has a pair of elevators. These control surfaces are made with tiny scissors snips as shown below.

Rudder

The creased body of the T-Wing has a stabilizing effect. Like the fin of a commercial aircraft, this surface helps keep the craft going straight ahead.

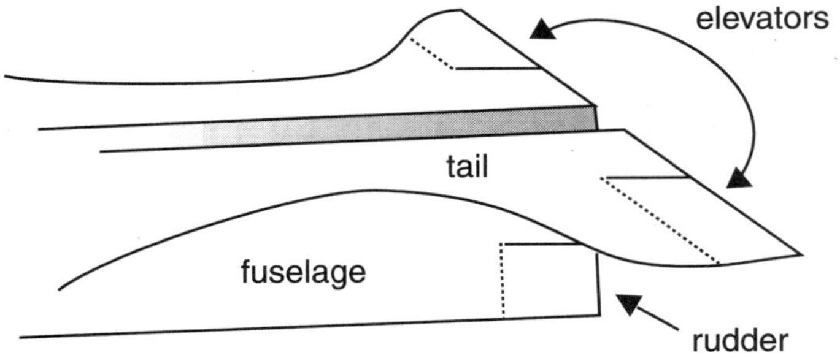

One snip of the scissors is all that is needed to add a *rudder*. A rudder is a control surface that makes the craft turn right or left. When the rudder is bent out to the right, air striking its surface from the front pushes the tail to the left. This causes the plane's nose to turn to the right. Likewise, when the rudder is bent out to the left, air striking its surface from the front pushes the tail to the right. This causes the plane to turn to the left.

Ailerons

The T-Wing has another type of control surface called an *aileron*. Ailerons are found on the wings' trailing edge. To build your aileron tabs, use scissors to make the snip shown below.

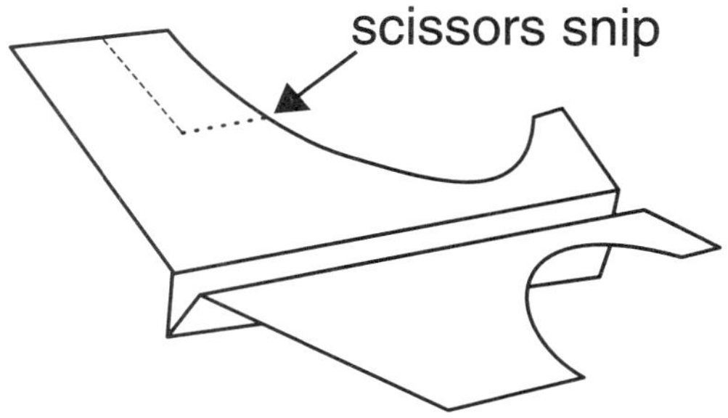

Ailerons cause the plane to tilt or *bank*. When a wing's aileron is raised, air pushes against it, causing that wing to dip.

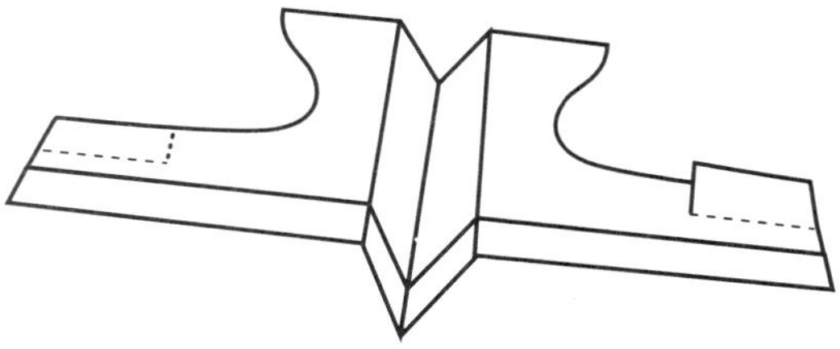

When a wing dips, the plane turns toward the lowered side. Although ailerons can turn a plane by themselves, most of the time the rudder and the ailerons work together.

Taking Off

Now that you have some experience with flying gliders, it's time to create your own flight path. Set the rudder, ailerons, and elevator so that the glider flies a large circular path and returns to where it was launched. Think you can do it? Give it a try! Once you've accomplished this stunt, set the control surfaces so that the glider turns upside down in a big loop before returning to its starting point.

The Delta-1

The Concorde is a supersonic jet that flies faster than all other commercial jets. To attain high-speed flight, the Concorde has a special design. Its wings have a triangle shape. This wing shape is known as a *delta wing*. It was named after the Greek letter *delta* which looks like this Δ.

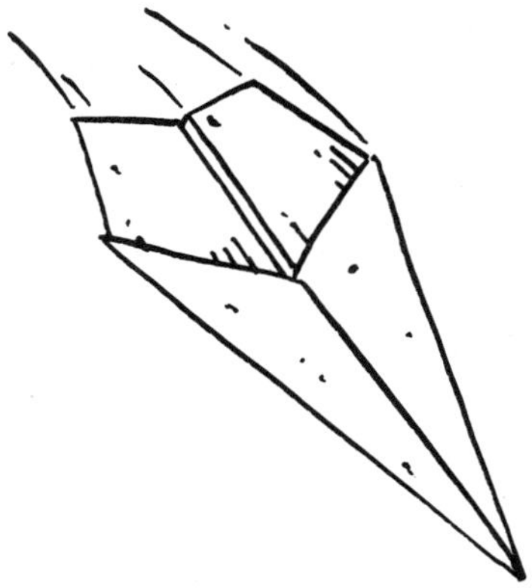

The Delta-1 glider is a basic design that probably has flown in every school lunch room! After you build it, however, you're going to add some control surfaces, and use it to explore some principles of flight. You'll even get a chance to build a second one that has some different flight characteristics.

Materials

- **Delta-1 Blackline Master, page 65**
- **scissors**
- **tape**

To Build:

1. Turn to the Plane Patterns section at the back of this book. Photocopy the **Delta-1** pattern on page 65.

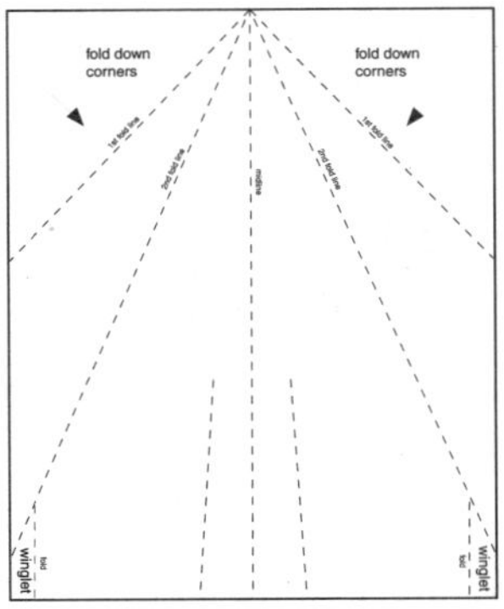

2. Fold along the first fold line to form a pointed nose.

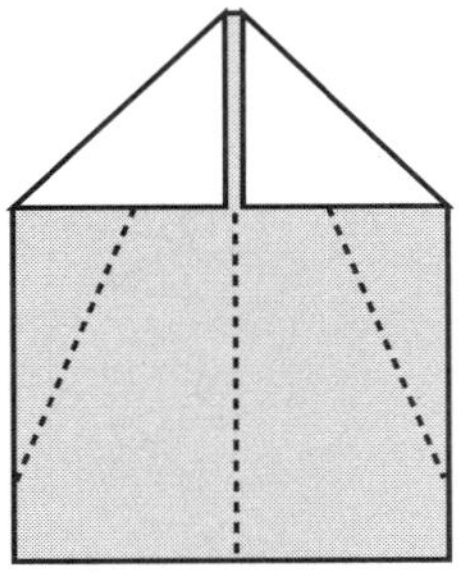

3. Fold along the second fold line to meet the center line.

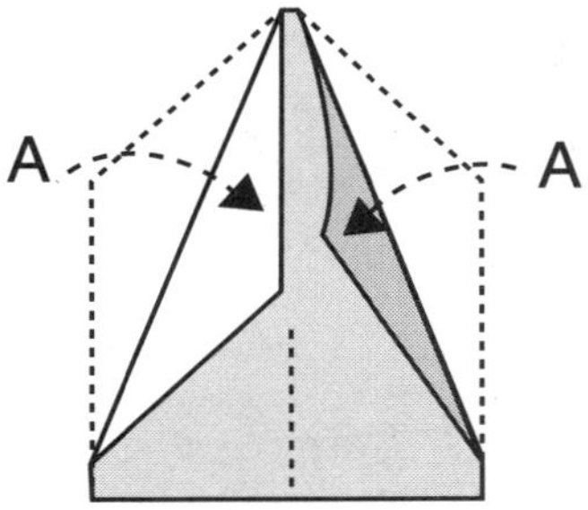

4. Fold the pattern in half lengthwise on the midline.

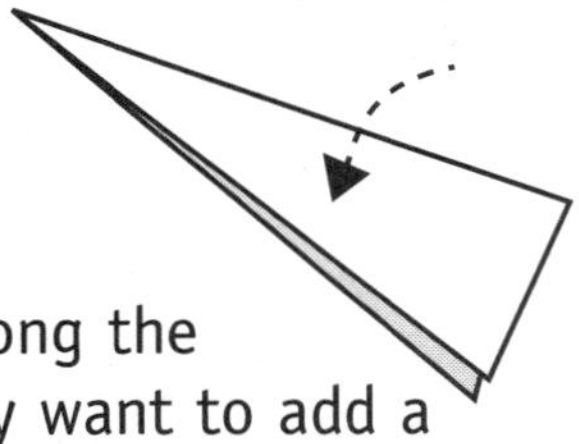

5. Bend out the wings along the fuselage lines. You may want to add a piece of tape to keep the shape together. Place the tape so that it pins together the upper surfaces of the wings.

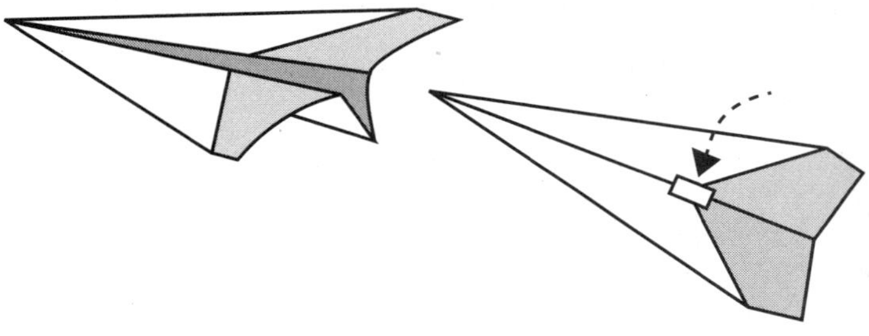

6. Bend up the winglets and your Delta-1 is ready to fly!

The Concorde can't have elevators because it doesn't have a stabilizer. Instead, it has six control surfaces called *elevons*. Three elevons are located on the trailing edge of each wing. The elevons, just like ailerons, can control the bank of the plane. They also act like elevators and control the climb angle.

You can add elevons by making two small cuts in the middle of the trailing edge on both wings.

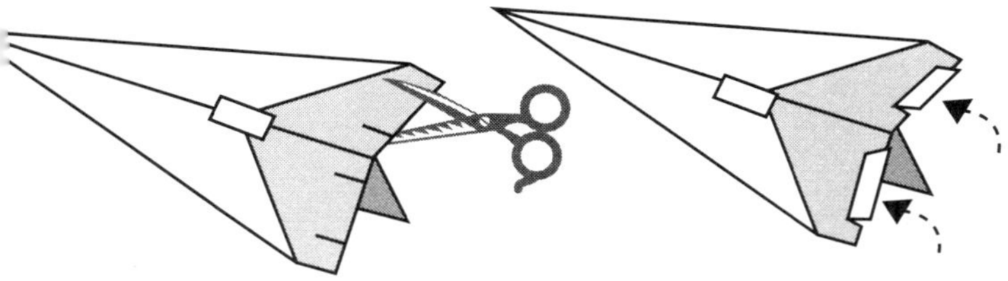

You can also add a rudder by making two short cuts on the back of the tail section.

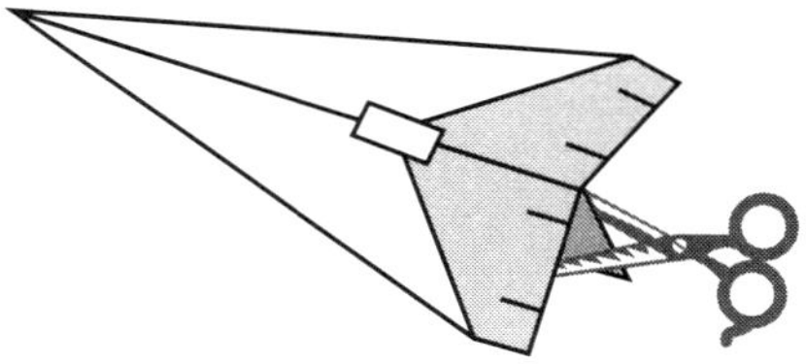

Test Flight

Once you've added the control surfaces, try flying the Delta-1.

Flying Facts

Extending and Contracting the Concorde's Delta Wing

Like other delta-wing jets, the Concorde's wing can extend and retract. When flying at high speeds, the wing is retracted. When traveling at slower speeds for landing and takeoff, the wing is extended.

When the wing is extended, it produces additional lift. This extra lift is needed at takeoff, since the jet hasn't accelerated to its high speed. The extra lift is also needed when the plane slows for landing.

When the wing is retracted, the Concorde becomes more streamlined. This shape has less resistance and moves much faster through the atmosphere. Since the Concorde travels at a very high speed, plenty of air strikes the smaller wing, so enough lift is created to keep the jet aloft.

Taking Off

By changing the angles of your folds, you can create delta gliders with differing amounts of wing surface area. Take a look at the two drawings of gliders below. Which one represents the Concorde when it is landing or taking off? Which one represents the Concorde flying at maximum speed? Although they are paper models, they can be used to study how wing shape affects speed and flight duration. Which one will fly faster? Which flies longer at a slower speed? How could you test your predictions?

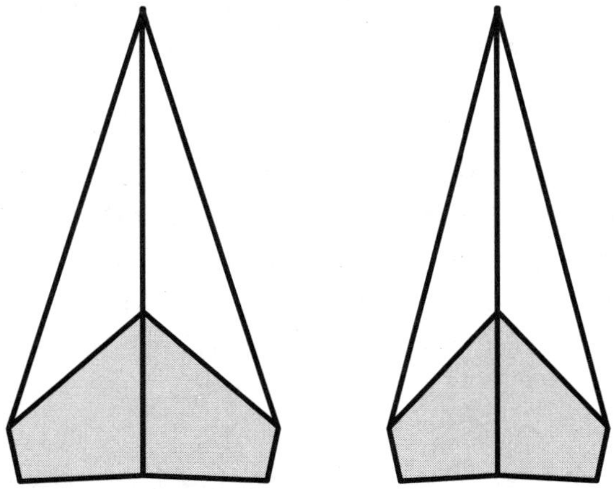

The Tray Bien

Here's how to build a simple glider from a plastic foam meat tray. Not only is this a great stunt glider, but it can survive many more crashes than a paper craft can.

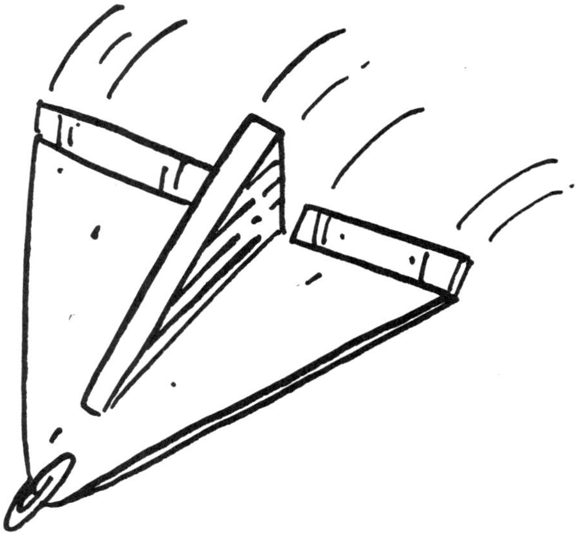

Materials

- plastic foam meat tray
- scissors
- paper clips
- tape

To Build:

1. Cut out the largest possible square from a plastic foam meat tray.
2. Mark the midline of one of the sides. Use a marker to draw lines from that point to both of the opposite corners.

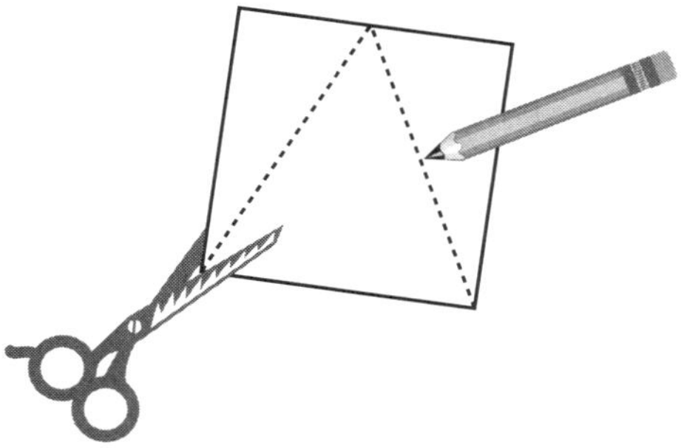

3. Use scissors to cut out the resulting large triangle. It will form the wing. One of the remaining small triangles will form the *fuselage*, or body.
4. Use scissors to slot and trim the pieces as shown here.

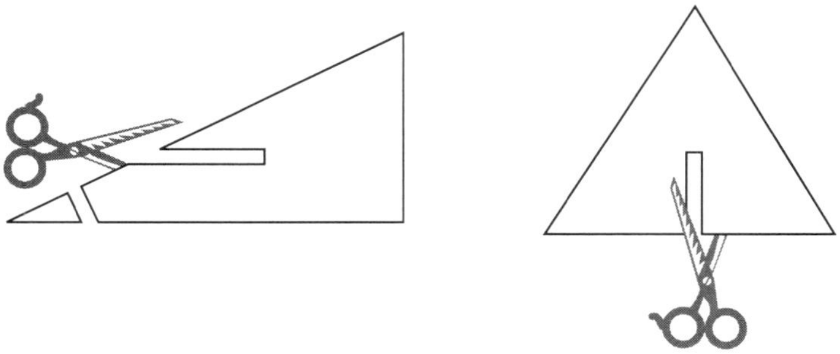

5. Insert the large wing triangle into the smaller fuselage triangle. The fit should be snug. Secure the pieces with a piece of tape.

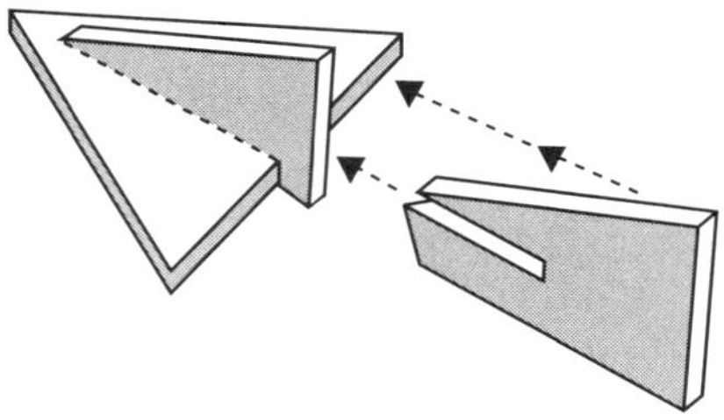

6. Use large paper clips to weigh down the nose. Otherwise, the glider will become unstable due to the wing's considerable lifting force.

7. Test your glider. If it dives, use a smaller paper clip. If it stalls, add more weight by adding paper clips.

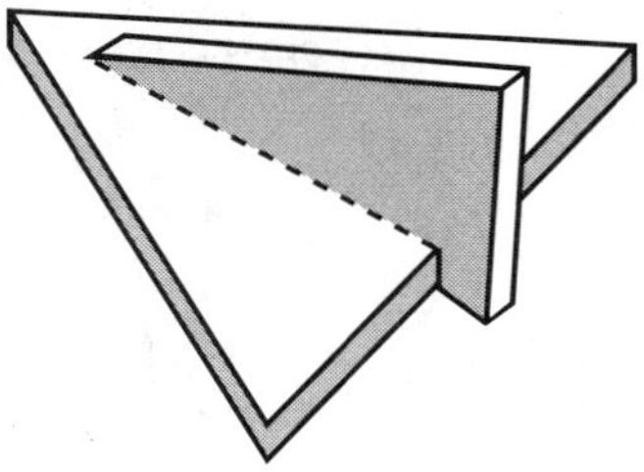

Extra Control

You can easily add a rudder and elevons to the Tray Bien. The rudder takes shape by simply placing a bend in the tail section of the fuselage. The elevons, like those in the delta glider, are made with small snips of the scissors. The control tab is then creased as shown.

Not Your Ordinary Glider

The Straw de Loop

Admit it. You've probably blasted dozens of paper straw covers into the cafeteria sky. But did you know that the straw itself can make a great flying thing? Just attach two paper loops and you'll create a stable flier that stays aloft for smooth, extended glides.

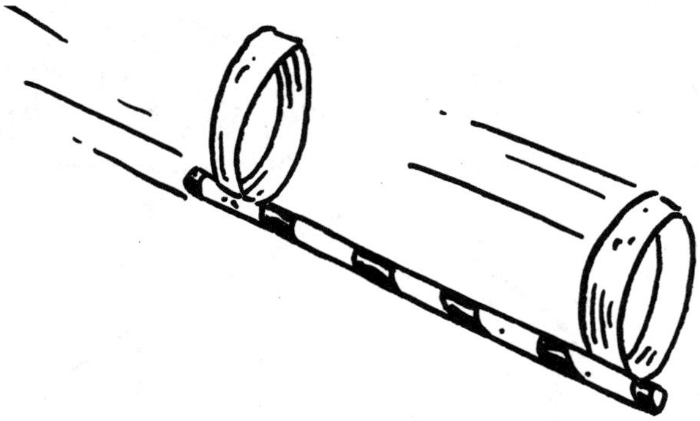

Materials

- Straw de Loop Blackline Master, page 67
- straw
- tape
- scissors

To Build:

1. Turn to the Plane Patterns section at the back of this book. Photocopy the **Straw de Loop** pattern on page 67.

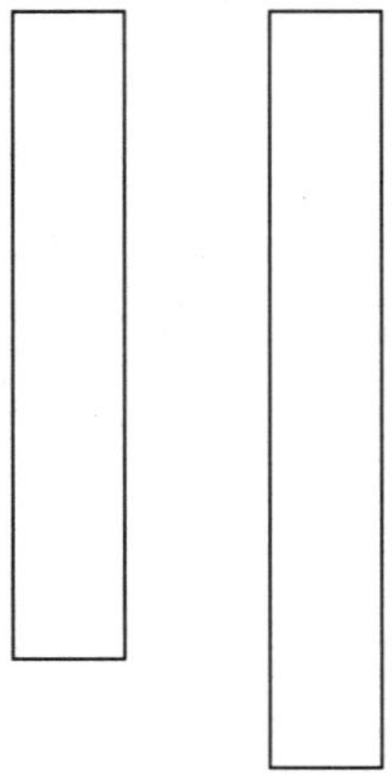

2. Cut out the two wing strips from the Straw de Loop pattern.
3. Bend each strip of paper into a loop. Overlap the ends by about one-half inch. Then secure with a piece of tape.
4. Place one loop at each end of a straw as shown here. Use tape to secure the loops to the straw.

Launching the Straw de Loop

To fly this glider, hold it by the middle of the straw. The small loop should be positioned at the front of the craft.

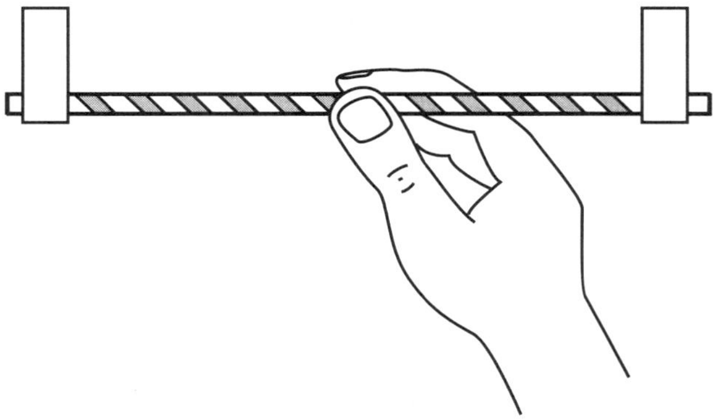

Gently toss the glider. If the craft dives, move the large loop forward. If the craft wobbles, move the small loop back. When the loops are just right, the craft will glide in a long, gently sloping path.

The Flying Napkin

Watch out for flying napkins! No, these aren't the after-dinner kind formed from crumpled balls of tissue. These Flying Napkins have a special construction that produces odd, but stable, fliers.

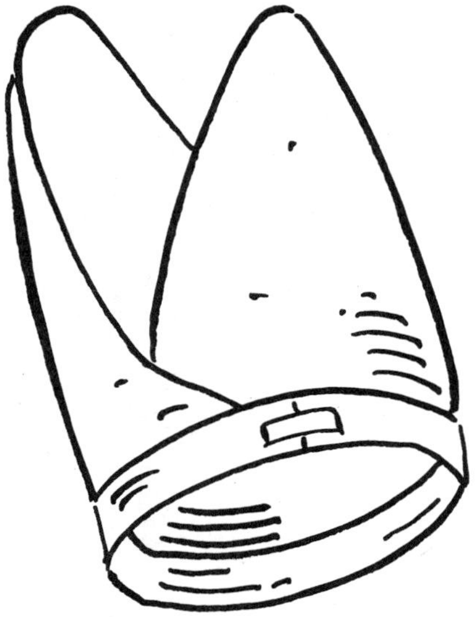

Materials

- **Flying Napkin Blackline Master, page 69**
- **tape**

To Build:

1. Turn to the Plane Patterns section at the back of this book. Photocopy the **Flying Napkin** pattern on page 69.

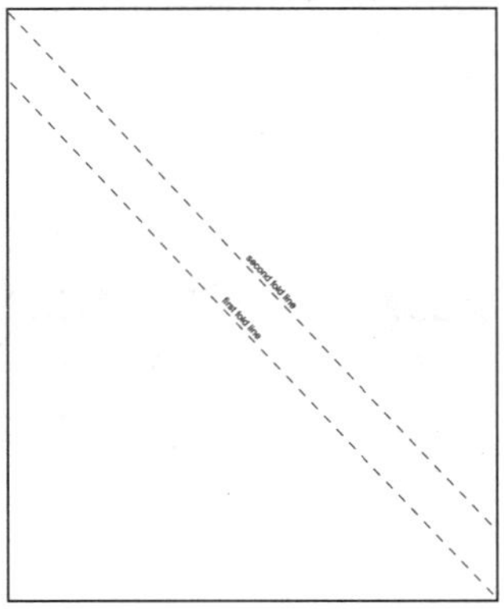

2. Fold the pattern along the first fold line as shown below.

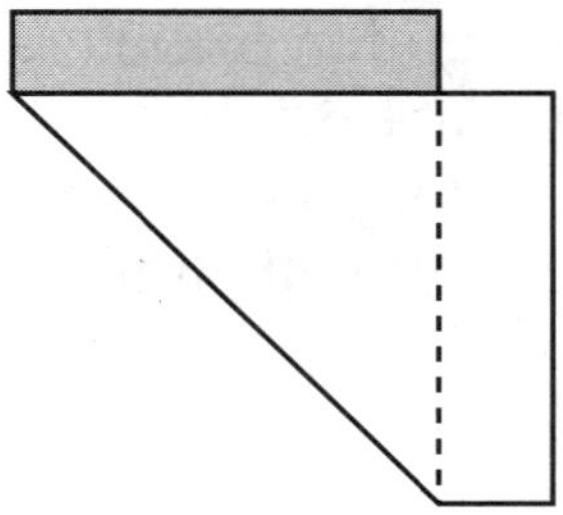

3. Now, fold along the second fold line. This will form an edge about one-half inch wide.

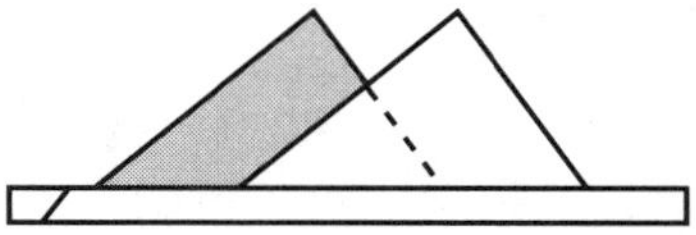

4. Curl the sheet into a cylindrical shape. Use tape to secure the craft.

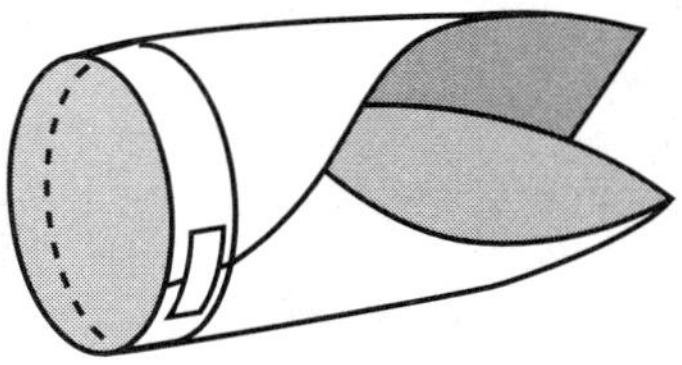

Launching the Flying Napkin

The Flying Napkin can be launched in several ways. The basic launch begins with you holding the glider in the middle of the body. Position the folded edge away from you. Then, with a gentle toss, the glider should be on its way.

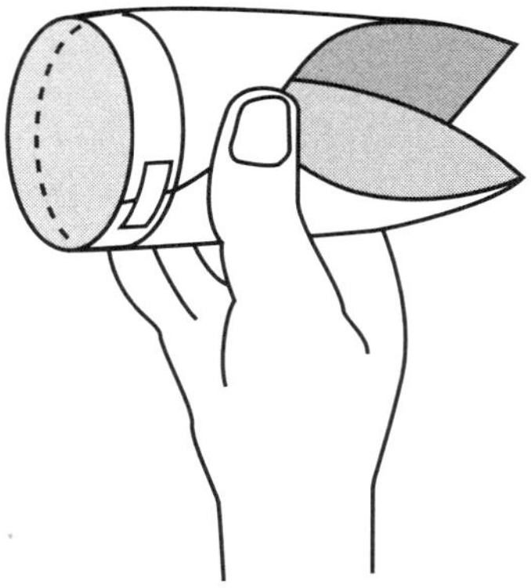

One of the more interesting launches is the backwards fling. To get the craft aloft, hold the back end of the glider with the cut edge facing up. Then, fold back your wrist, so the glider is facing backwards. A quick flick of the wrist sends your glider sailing on a long and stable voyage. Bon voyage!

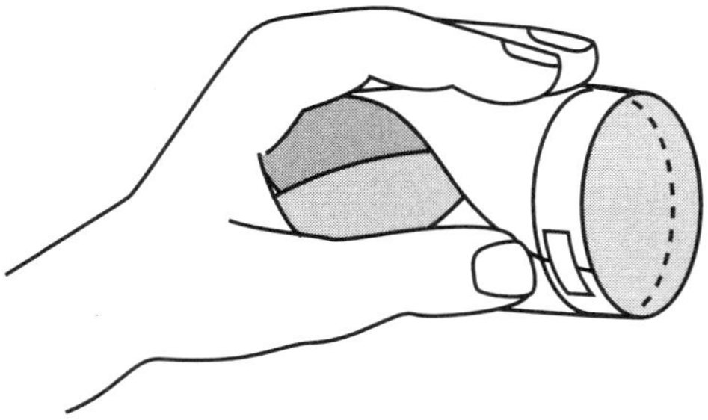

The Boomerang

Does a boomerang really return to its thrower? Why not build one to find out?

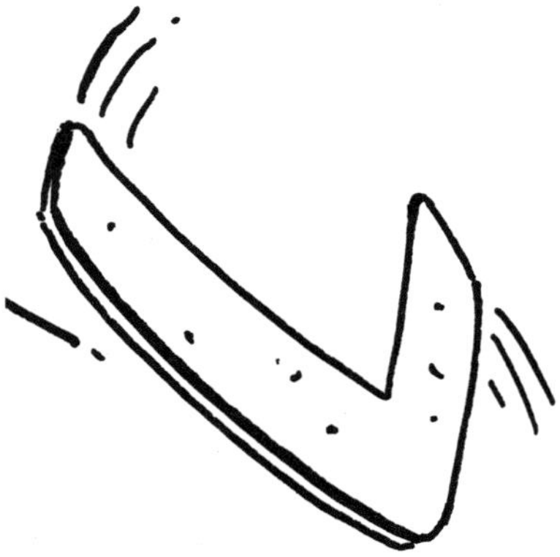

Materials

- Boomerang Blackline Master, page 71
- cardboard stock (such as cereal or clothes box sides)
- scissors
- paste

To Build:

1. Turn to the Plane Patterns section at the back of this book. Photocopy the **Boomerang** pattern on page 71.

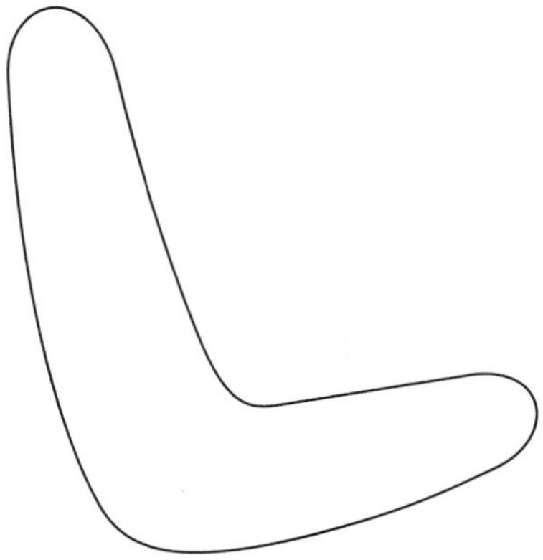

2. Cut out the Boomerang pattern.
3. Trace around the pattern four times on a piece of heavy cardstock. The cardboard of a clothes box or a cereal box makes a perfect boomerang.
4. Glue the four boomerangs together. Once the glue dries, you're ready to practice throwing.

Throwing the Boomerang

❶ **Wear eye protection.** Hold the Boomerang firmly in one hand as shown.

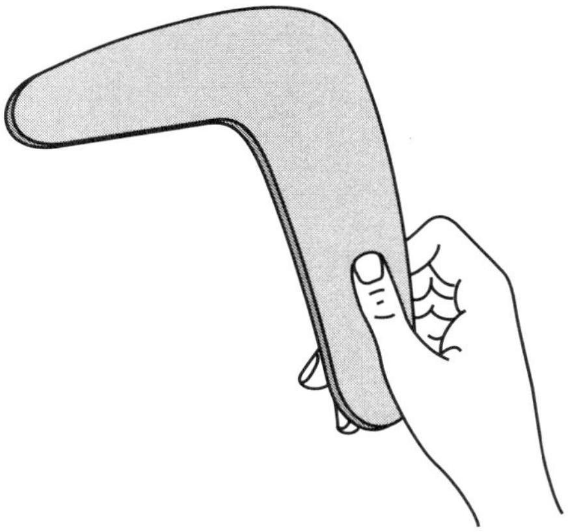

❷ Aim your throw steeply into any breeze or slight wind. Throw the Boomerang overhand. It should leave your hand with a good spin. When thrown correctly, the Boomerang will make a giant U-turn and return to you!

Taking Off

Find out how changing the angle and slope of the throw changes this craft's flight path! You can change the slope of your throw by aiming higher or lower. You can change the angle of your throw by changing the direction of the wind. Will the Boomerang return on days when there is no wind?

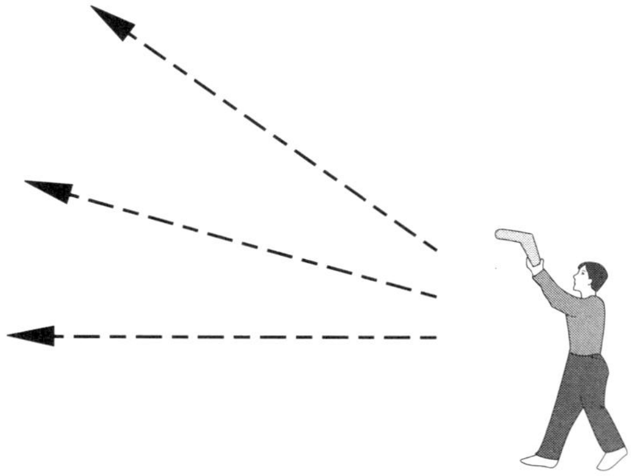

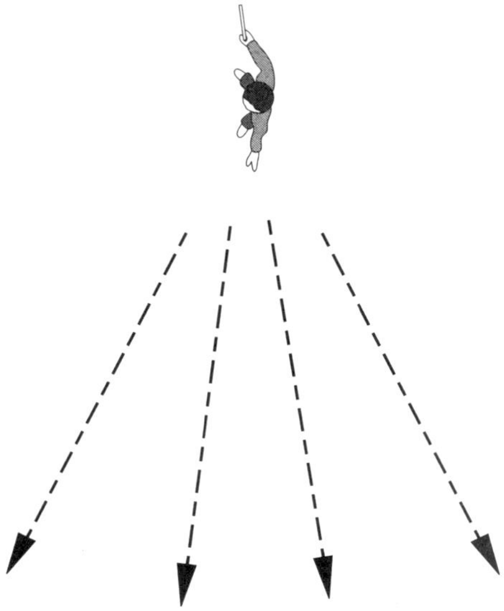

Flying Facts

Boomerangs of No Return

Imagine designing boomerangs to not return! Although this sounds hard to believe, it's true. Most cultures that used the boomerang as a weapon designed it for one-way trips. The use of one-way boomerangs in hunting and warfare can be traced to origins in Australia, Egypt, India, and the American Southwest. One type of boomerang, however, was built to return. This round-trip weapon was used by native Australian cultures during bird hunts. Can you guess why?

The Parachute

Over one hundred years before the first plane ever flew, people were jumping out of the sky. It all started in 1797, when Andre-Jacques Gamerin jumped from a hot air balloon wearing a parachute. As he had hoped, the parachute brought him safely and gently to the ground. Soon after, his daughter Eliza became the first woman parachutist.

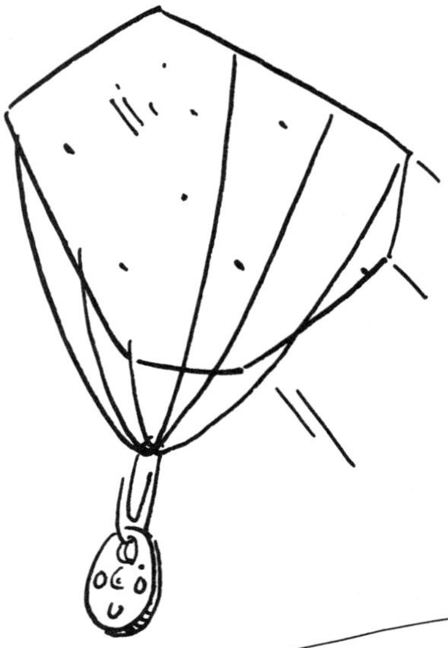

Materials

- Parachute Blackline Master, page 73
- thread (or kite string)
- plastic garbage bag
- centimeter ruler
- scissors
- tape
- small toy (cargo)
- paper clip

To Build:

1. Turn to the Plane Patterns section at the back of this book. Photocopy the **Parachute** pattern on page 73.

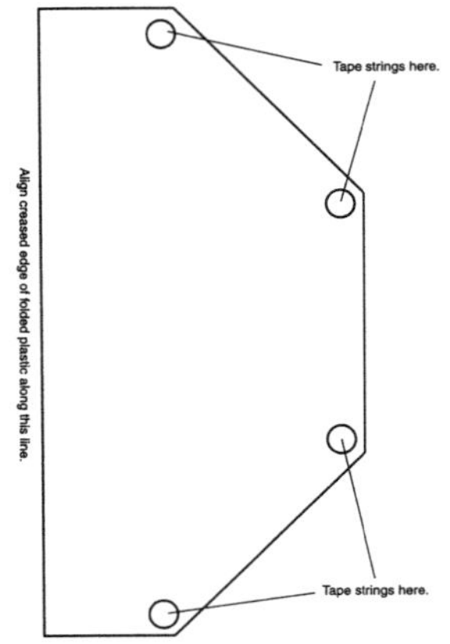

2. Use scissors to slit open the sides and bottom of a plastic garbage bag. Then, cut out a square that measures 20 centimeters on each side. Fold the square in half.

3. Place the pattern over the folded plastic. Use your scissors to cut off the corners of the plastic.

4. Unfold the plastic into the octagon pattern shown here. Cut out a hole about the size of a quarter in the center of the Parachute.

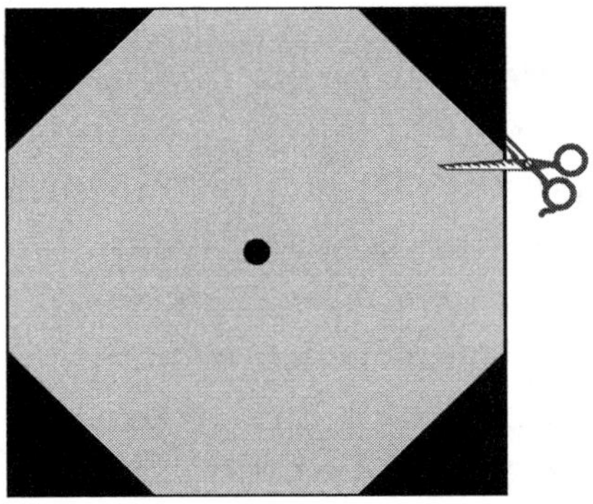

5. Cut four lengths of string, each about 30 centimeters long.

❻ Use tape to attach the strings to the Parachute. The ends of each string should be attached to two consecutive corners.

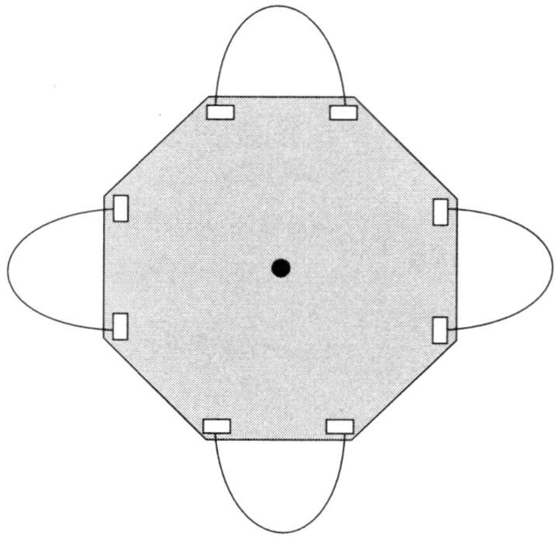

❼ Slide all four loops around a paper clip to bring them together. Attach a parachuting doll, some sort of cutout, or other object of weight to the paper clip.

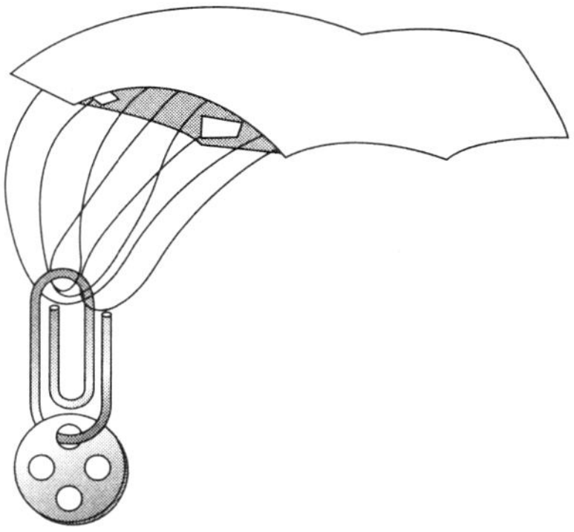

Launching the Parachute

❶ Like a real parachutist, you'll first need to "pack the chute." To do so, fold the plastic parachute in half. Then, fold this double thickness in half.

❷ Fold the double-folded chute into a finger-sized pack.

❸ Wind the strings around the folded chute.

❹ Toss the chute with attached weight skyward.

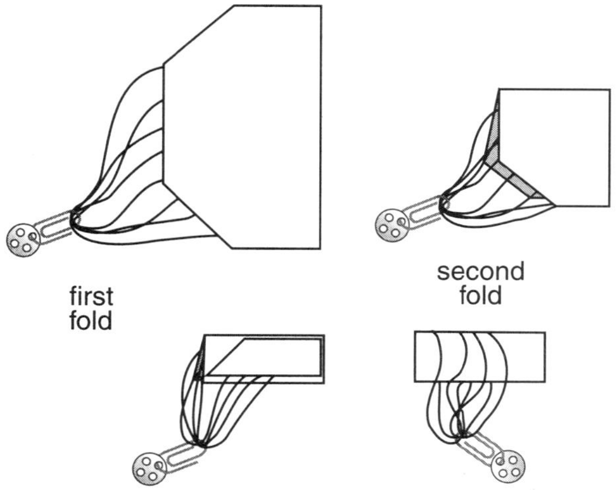

Flying Facts

Holes in the Chute

Air that is trapped under a parachute's canopy tends to escape in large, uneven rushes. This movement causes the parachute to sway. To reduce the swaying, a small hole can be cut into the top of the chute. This hole permits air to escape in a steady, even flow.

The Paraglide

More than 500 years ago, Leonardo da Vinci drew the plans for a parachute. His early design looked like a pyramid.

Materials

- Paraglide Blackline Master, page 75
- plastic garbage bag
- thread (or kite string)
- three straws
- scissors
- tape
- several large paper clips

At the end of the eighteenth century, a slightly different design appeared. It had a circular canopy that looked like an umbrella. Ropes, called shroud lines, were tied from the edge of the canopy to the parachutist below.

Nowadays, there are many different parachute designs. Like wings, some of the parachutes develop lift. This extra lift, produced by certain canopy designs, gives the parachutist a much longer ride.

To Build:

1. Turn to the Plane Patterns section at the back of this book. Photocopy the **Paraglide** pattern on page 75.

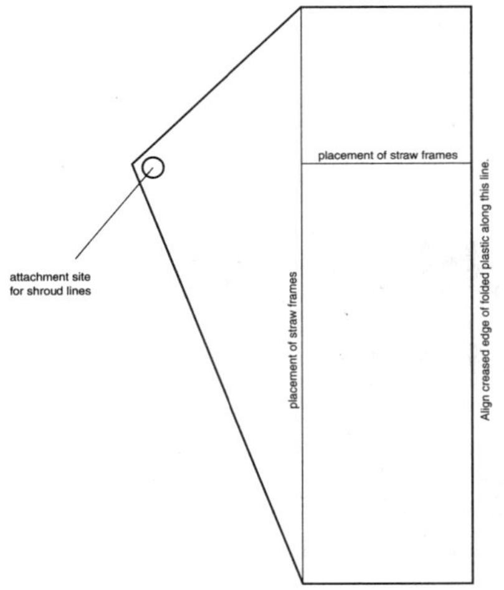

2. Use scissors to cut out the pattern.

3. Place this pattern along one of the folded edges of a plastic garbage bag. Use your scissors to cut through the double thickness of the bag. When you unfold the bag, you should have a pattern that looks like this:

4. Position the three straws on the unfolded plastic as shown below. Trim the straw lengths as needed.

5. Tape the straws to the pattern.

6. Use tape to attach a 30-centimeter length of string to the spots marked on the pattern. This string will form a loop upon which the paper clips will hang.

7. Hang several large paper clips on the string. You can use tape to attach additional objects if more weight is needed.

Test Flight

Hold out the Paraglide and release. Like a parachute, the Paraglide's large surface area will trap air, increasing the effect of air resistance. This resistance will slow the Paraglide's descent. In addition, the winglike shape allows the Paraglide to descend more like a glider than a simple parachute.

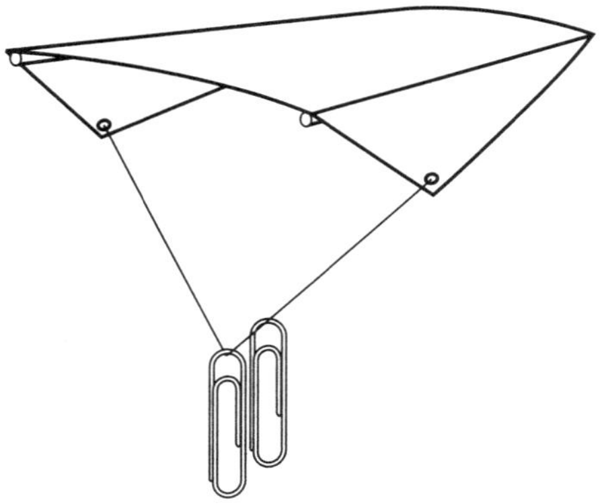

The Balloon Rocket

When a balloon is inflated, its rubber skin is stretched. Just like a twisted rubber band, this stretched material stores energy.

When the balloon neck is released, the air is allowed to escape. The stored energy is used to force air out of the open balloon neck. The escaping air sends the balloon moving in the opposite direction.

You can explore balloon power with the following activity.

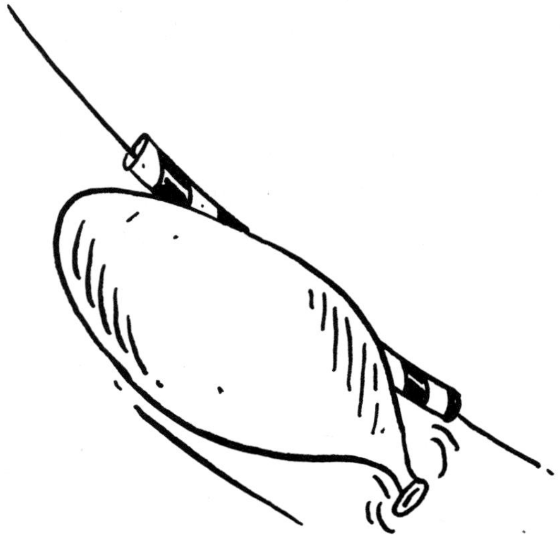

Materials

- balloon
- straw
- kite string
- scissors
- tape

To Build:

1. Thread a long string through a straw.
2. Tie both ends of the string to objects on opposites sides of the room such as chairs or table legs. Make sure that the string is fully stretched and tight.

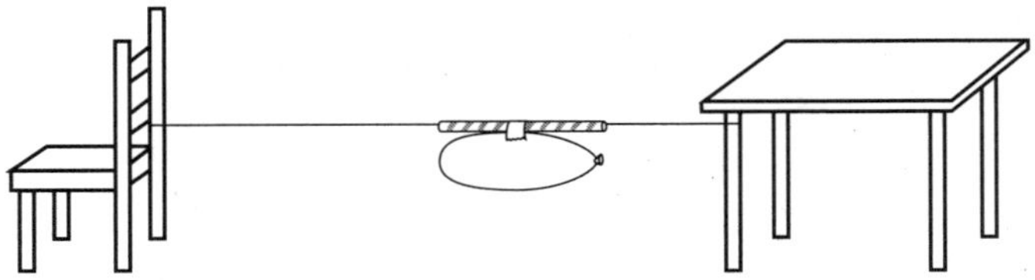

3. Inflate a balloon and hold its neck closed. Use tape to attach this balloon to the straw.

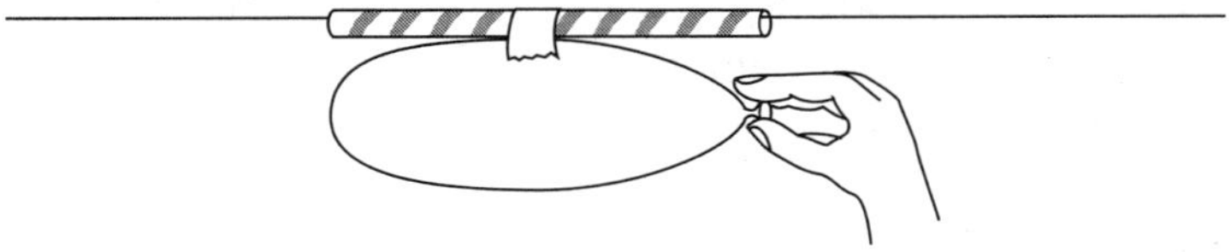

Launching the Balloon Rocket

Once it is attached, release the neck and watch the Balloon Rocket fly along the track.

Taking Off

How can you increase the distance that this Balloon Rocket travels? After you have thought about it, redesign your Balloon Rocket and try again.

Pushing the Envelope

The Dragonfly

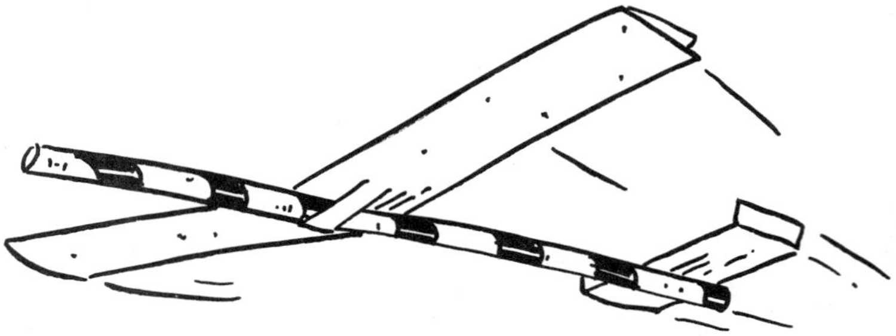

The Dragonfly is a glider whose wings have a half-teardrop shape called an airfoil. This glider also has a thin, but rigid, fuselage built with two straws. For now, you'll fly it as a glider. Later on, you'll get a chance to power this craft with a rocket engine.

Lift

Hold a thin strip of paper beneath your lower lip. Blow as hard as you can. What happens to the paper?

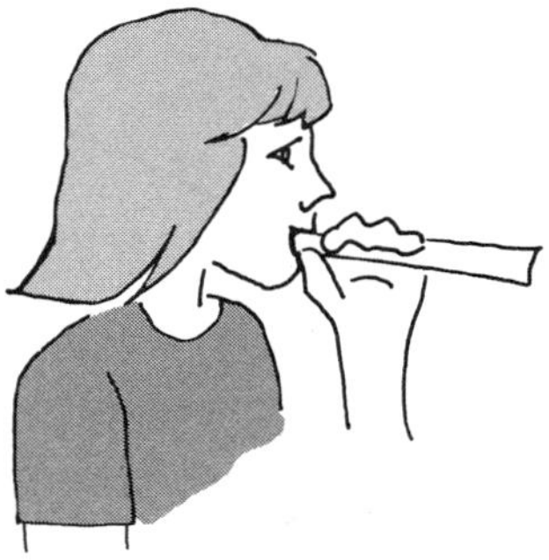

The paper rises because your blowing created an air stream that reduced the air pressure over the paper strip. The greater air pressure below the paper strip forced it up or lifted it. This lift was strong enough to overcome the weight of the paper. The strip rose because the upward force was greater than the downward force of the paper's weight.

Although the airfoil shape can improve a wing's efficiency, many scientists believe that the lift comes from deflection of air particles. As the bottom surface of the wing strikes air particles, it is exposed to a constant bombardment of force. It is this force that keeps the wing (and anything attached to it) up.

But you don't have to look at an aircraft's wing to observe this effect. If you've ever held your hand out in a strong wind, you probably noticed that you could create a "lift" by slightly raising your finger tips. Air striking your palm was deflected downward. At the same time, the force of this collision drove your hand upwards.

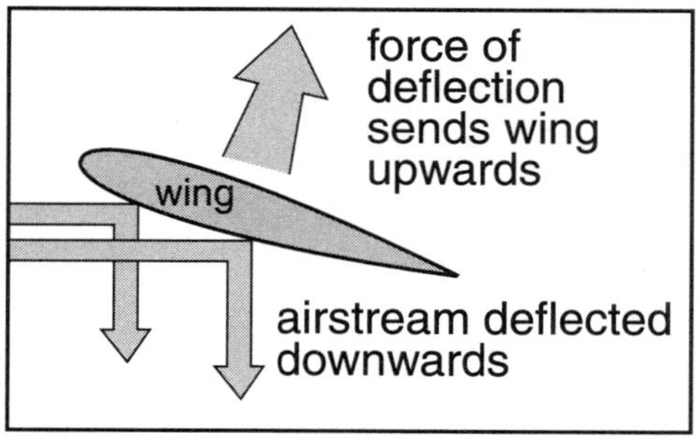

Flying Facts

De-icing Wings

During winter, plane wings must be de-iced. One reason for de-icing is to prevent ice from altering the streamline shape of the wing. The other reason is to remove the extra weight added by the ice buildup.

Materials

- **Dragonfly Blackline Master, page 77**
- **two straws**
- **scissors**
- **tape**
- **index card**
- **clay**

To Build:

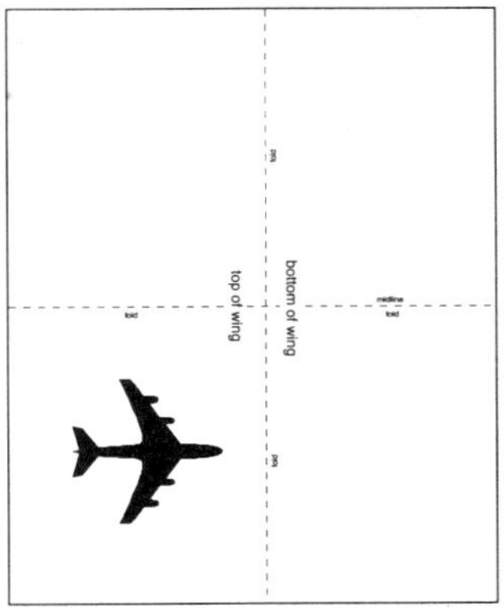

1. Turn to the Plane Patterns section at the back of this book. Photocopy the **Dragonfly** pattern on page 77.

2. Fold the wing along the vertical dashed line. Fold it so that the wing markings face the outside.

3. Place the folded wing down on a flat surface so that the word *Dragonfly* faces upward. Slide the upper surface toward the crease. It should buckle over the bottom section, producing a curved wing. Secure the wing's curved shape with a piece of tape. The tape should stretch the entire width of the wing's trailing edge.

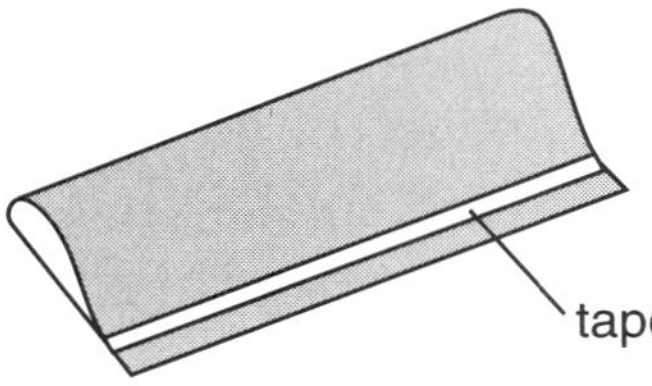

4. Once the airfoil shape is secured with tape, fold and crease the wing along its midline. Then, bend the right and left wing halves so that they form a shallow V-shape (as shown below).

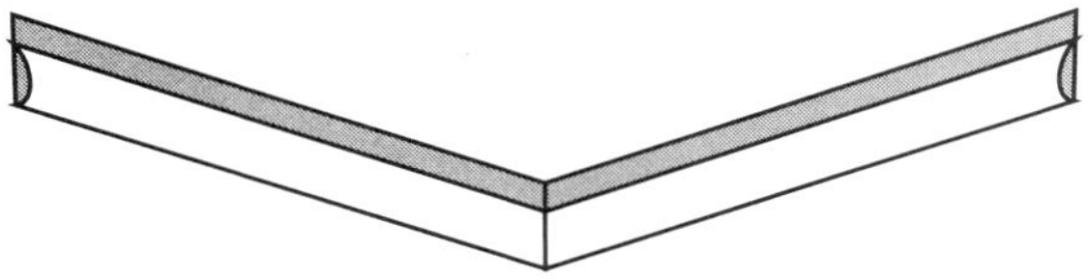

5. To make the fuselage, or body, insert one straw into another. To form a snug connection, you may have to twist the end of one straw to make it easier to slide into the other straw.

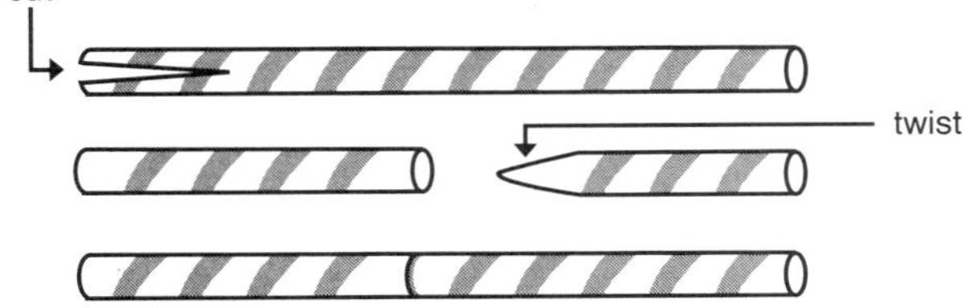

6. Use tape to attach the straw fuselage to the flat, or bottom, surface of the wing. The straw should be positioned along the wing's midline. The wing should be placed about 5 centimeters back from the front end of the straw.

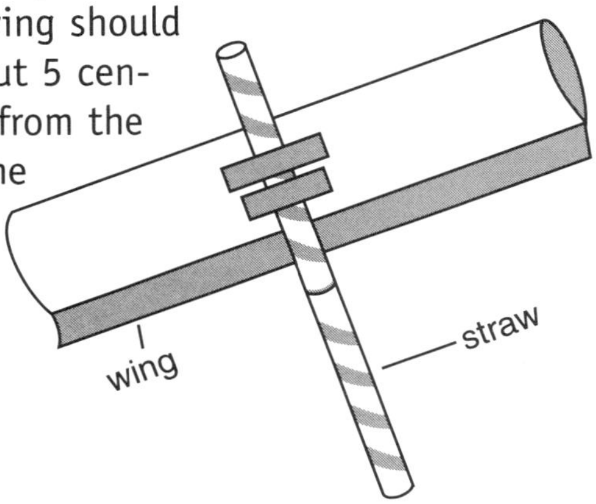

7. Bend up the edges of an index card so that it looks like this:

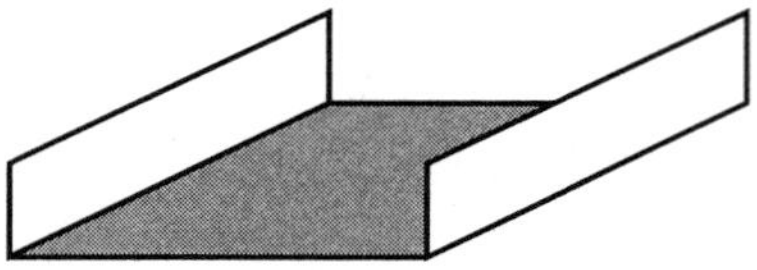

8. Use tape to secure the card to the end of the Dragonfly's tail.

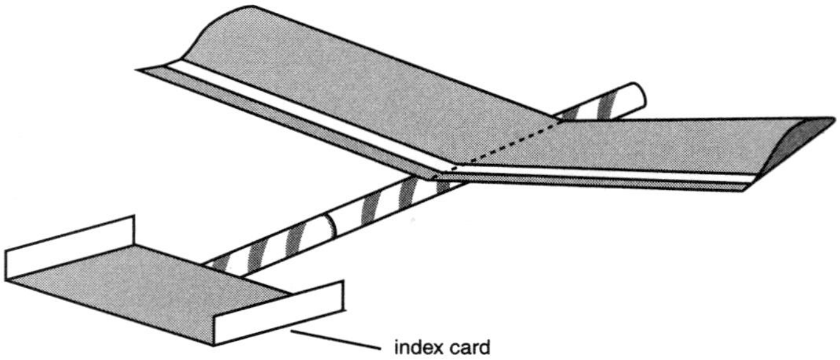

9. Add a pea-sized lump of clay to the nose of the glider. Now, check the balance point by supporting the glider with your finger. Add or take away clay so that the Dragonfly balances when your finger supports the craft from right under the middle of the wing.

Test Flight

Gently toss the Dragonfly. If it stalls, add more clay. If it dives, remove some clay.

Flying Facts

Flaps

Most aircraft have flaps. A flap is a control surface that changes the shape of the wing. When the flap is extended, the wing takes on extra curved area. This extra curved area produces additional lift. Flaps are used during takeoffs and landings. They add the extra lift needed to keep the aircraft aloft at slow speeds. The amount of flap is measured in degrees of flap angle. The greater the angle, the more extended the flap.

Taking Off

Do you think wing flaps would change the flight of the Dragonfly? Would their extra weight bring the craft down? Or would the extra curve keep the craft flying? Once you've made your prediction, construct two small flaps from strips of paper. Tape these strips to the trailing edges of the wings and test your prediction!

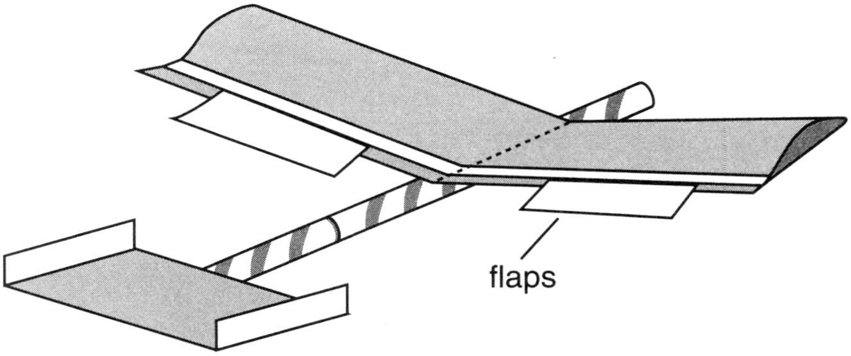

The Rocket-Powered Dragonfly

You can change the Dragonfly from a glider to a rocket-powered craft by attaching a balloon.

An inflated balloon is a great engine for "jet propulsion." The jet of escaping air can be harnessed by a glider and used to keep it aloft. It can even be used to launch the glider.

You can use all sorts of balloons for this power. The best ones, however, are the long sausage-shaped ones.

Before adding the rocket power, make sure that your Dragonfly is still securely held together. Patch up any tears or rips with small pieces of tape.

Balance

To find the right spot to attach the inflated balloon, you'll need to explore the balance of your craft. Select a spot on the fuselage that appears to be halfway down the length of the glider. Place your finger under this spot. Does the glider balance? If not, slide your finger in either direction until the Dragonfly balances. When you find the balancing point, use a marker to identify it.

Materials

- Dragonfly glider (built in previous activity)
- balloon
- straw
- small rubber band
- tape

To Build:

1. Use about a 6-inch (15-centimeter) length of tape to form a loop, sticky side facing outward. Press this tape loop along the balancing point marked on the straw fuselage.

2. To produce a slow, steady airstream, place a small section of straw in the opening of a balloon. Secure the straw with a rubber band. Make sure that the rubber band doesn't collapse the straw. Then, inflate the balloon halfway. Pinch the straw so that the air does not escape.

3. Press the middle of the balloon against the tape loop with enough pressure to stick the balloon to the bottom of the fuselage.

Test Flight

Countdown: 5 . . . 4 . . . 3 . . . 2 . . . 1. Release! With a lifting push, the Rocket-Powered Dragonfly should take off on its own power.

If needed, use clay to balance the Rocket-Powered Dragonfly.

Flying Facts

Rocket-Assisted Launch

Rocket power helps launch jets from the deck of aircraft carriers. This extra boost is part of a launching system that is part of the ship's deck. When fired, the rockets quickly accelerate the jet to takeoff speed. As the jet rises into the air, it detaches from the launch system. Within seconds, its only power is supplied by the onboard engines.

Mission Accomplished

"The captain has turned on the seat belt light indicating our final approach. We're just about to land."

By now, you've had quite a trip. Your tour of flying things has taken you from simple spinners to rocket-powered gliders. You've learned about all sorts of flight concepts such as lift, stalls, banks, and cambered wings. Chances are that you won't forget them. That's because instead of just reading about these concepts, you actually built aircraft and tested them.

Now, however, it's up to you. Use your imagination to dream up new creations. Try designing and testing new types of aircraft.
Remember, the sky's the limit!

Before you go, however, don't forget your wings. You've earned them.

Congratulations!

Glossary

aileron A hinged wing section that causes a plane to bank

airfoil A shape with a curved upper surface and flat lower surface that can increase the efficiency of a wing

bank The tipping of an aircraft that is produced when one wing is raised while the other is lowered

camber The curve of the airfoil shape

climb An aircraft's nose goes up and the plane ascends

control surface A hinged aircraft part that can extend into the airstream, affecting the craft's flight path

delta wing Triangular shaped wing

dive An aircraft's nose goes down and the plane descends

elevator A hinged part of the stabilizer that controls the up-and-down position of the aircraft's nose

elevons Extendible control surfaces that are found on delta wings

fin The vertical part of an aircraft's tail that prevents the craft from swaying side to side

flap Extendible surfaces that change the shape of an aircraft's wing

flap angle A measurement of how much the flap has altered the wing shape

fuselage The body of an aircraft

gravity The force that pulls all objects towards the earth's center

horizontal stabilizer *(stabilizer)* This sideways surface keeps the nose of an aircraft from bouncing up and down.

leading edge The edge of the wing that faces the front of an aircraft

lift The upward force that counteracts gravity

nose The front part of an aircraft

pitch The angle at which the blades of a propeller "cut" through the air

propeller *(prop)* An "air screw" whose spinning motion propels the plane forward

rudder A hinged portion of the upright tail section that helps turn an aircraft right or left

shaft A rod that fits snugly into the propeller

shroud lines The lines that connect the fabric canopy of a parachute to its hanging cargo

stability A balance that results when opposing forces cancel each other out

stabilizer The horizontal part of an aircraft's tail section. It helps keep the craft's nose from bobbing up and down.

stall A loss of lift that can occur when an aircraft climbs too steeply

tail The rear part of an aircraft

trailing edge The edge of the wing that faces the rear of an aircraft

vertical stabilizer *(fin)* This up-and-down surface prevents an aircraft from sloshing back and forth

weight The force with which an object is attracted by the earth

winglets The bent-up tips of an aircraft's wings which produce additional stability

wing tab Control surface on the wing of an aircraft that can be extended in order to adjust the flight path

Plane Patterns

The Papercopter

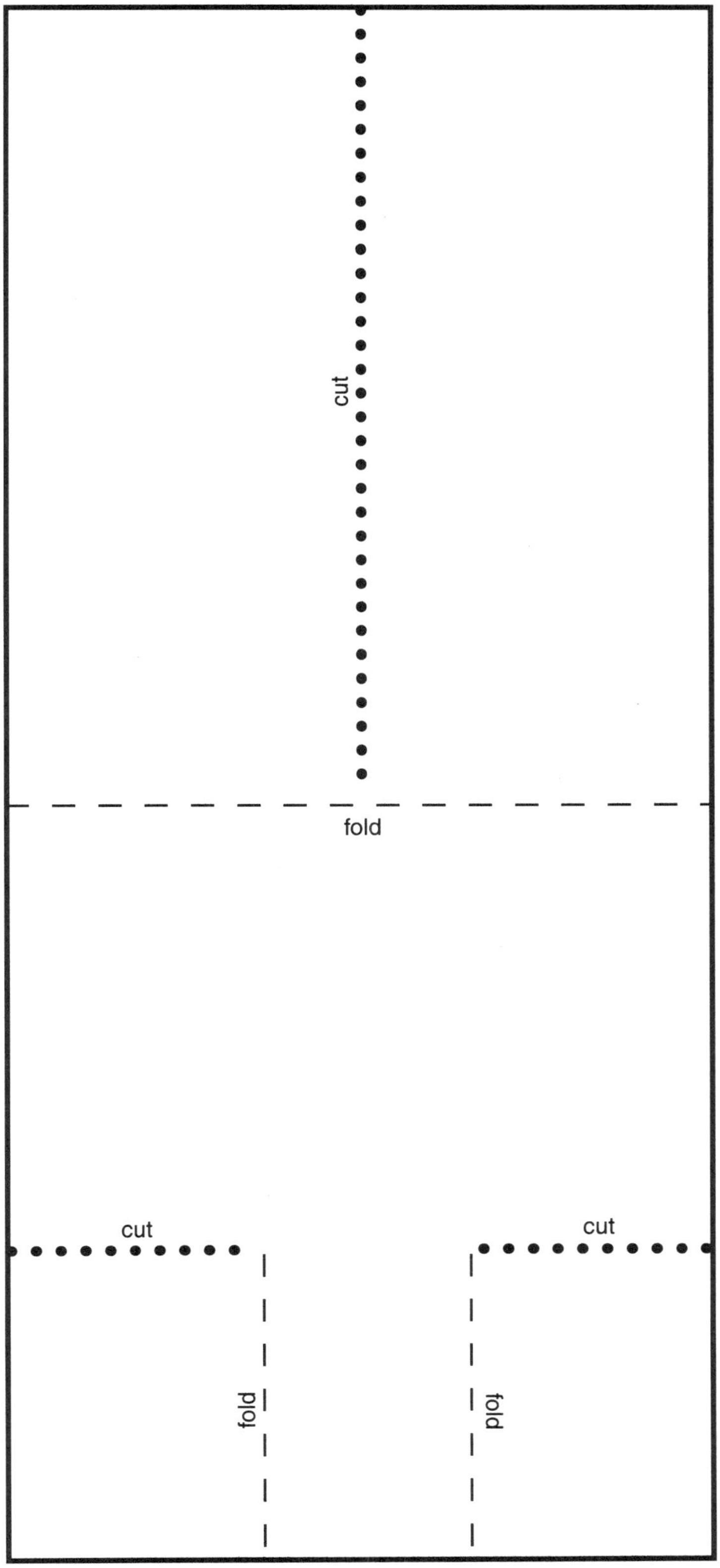

The Flutter Faller

The Circling Cylinder

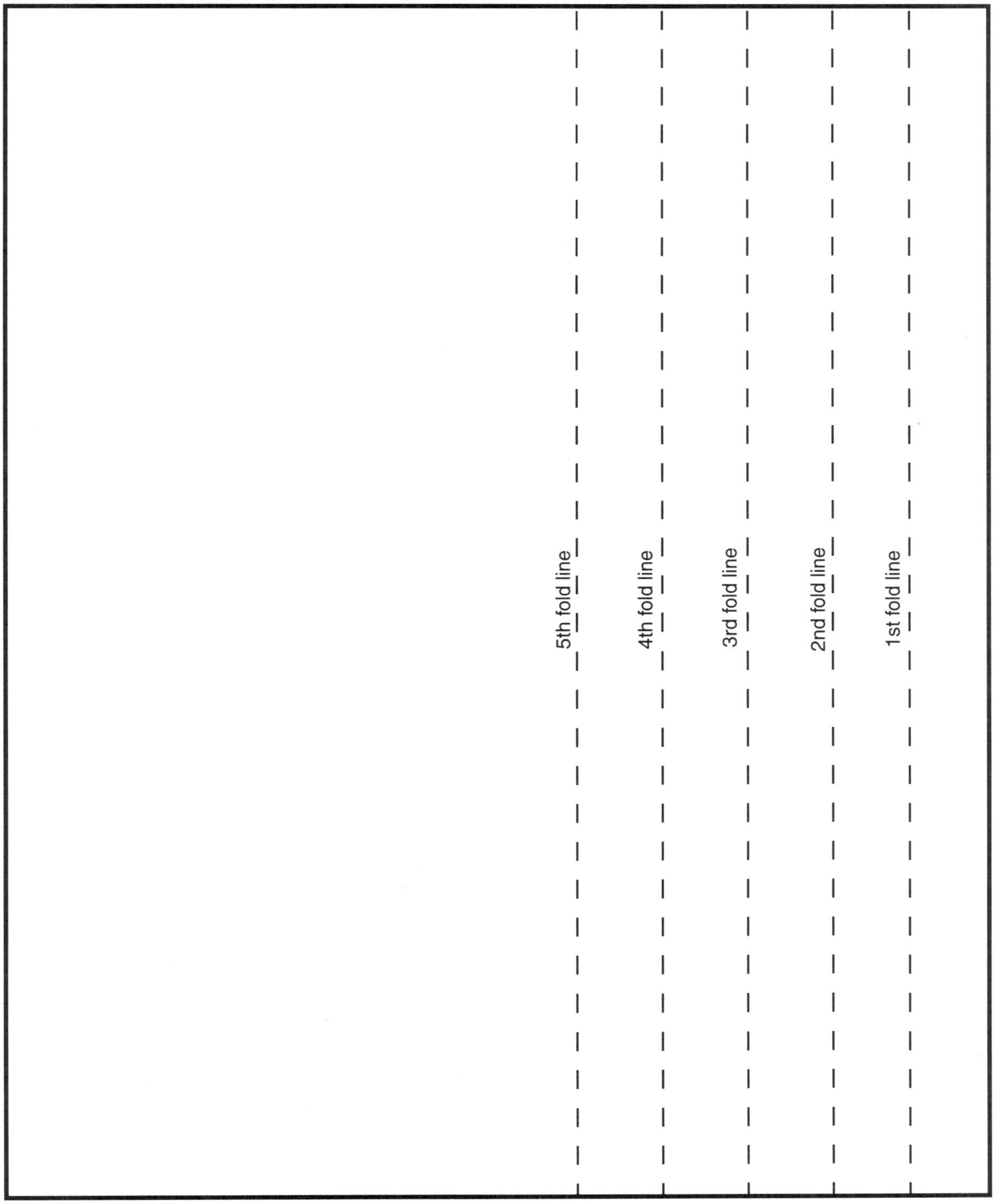

The Flying Wing

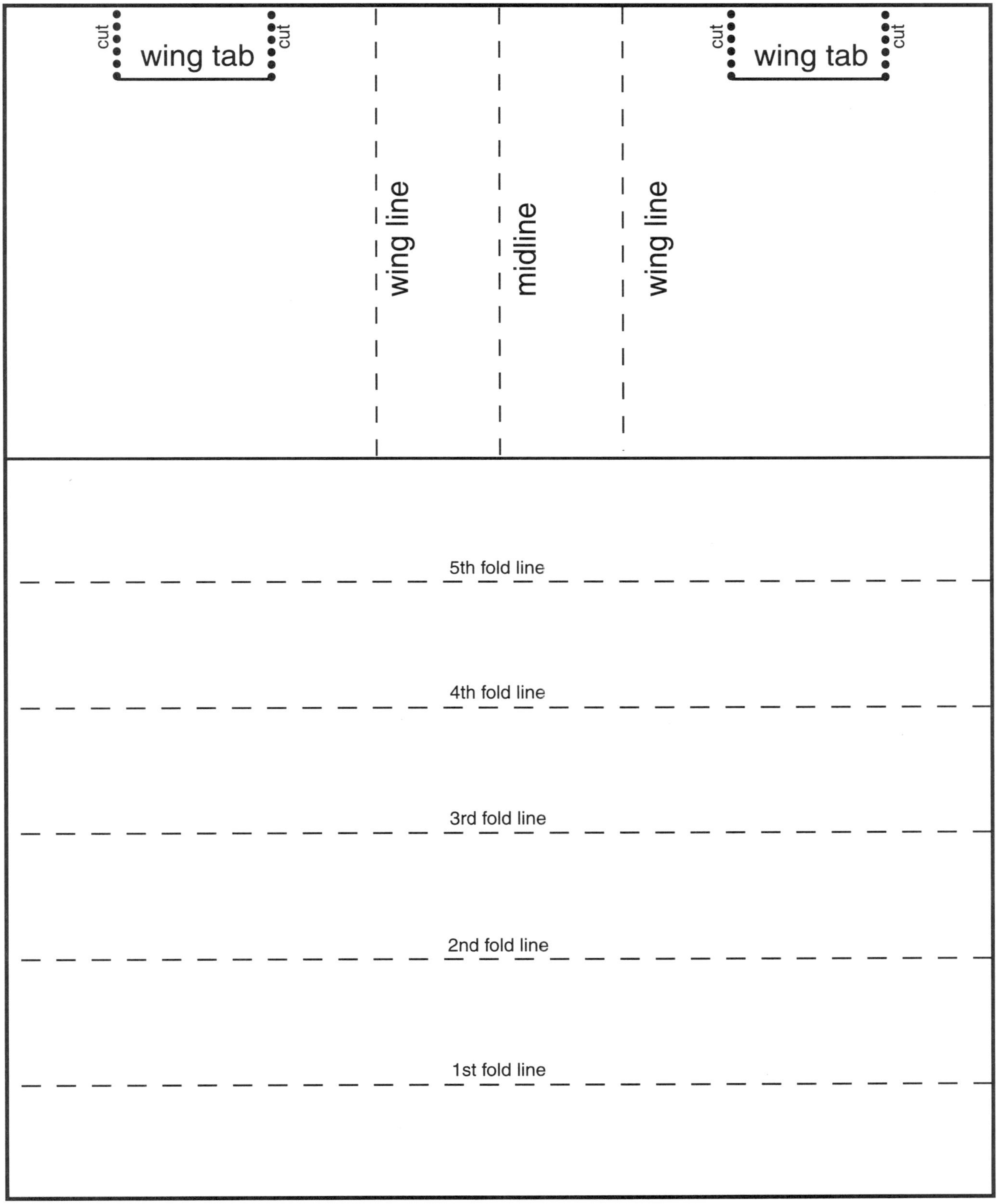

The Osprey

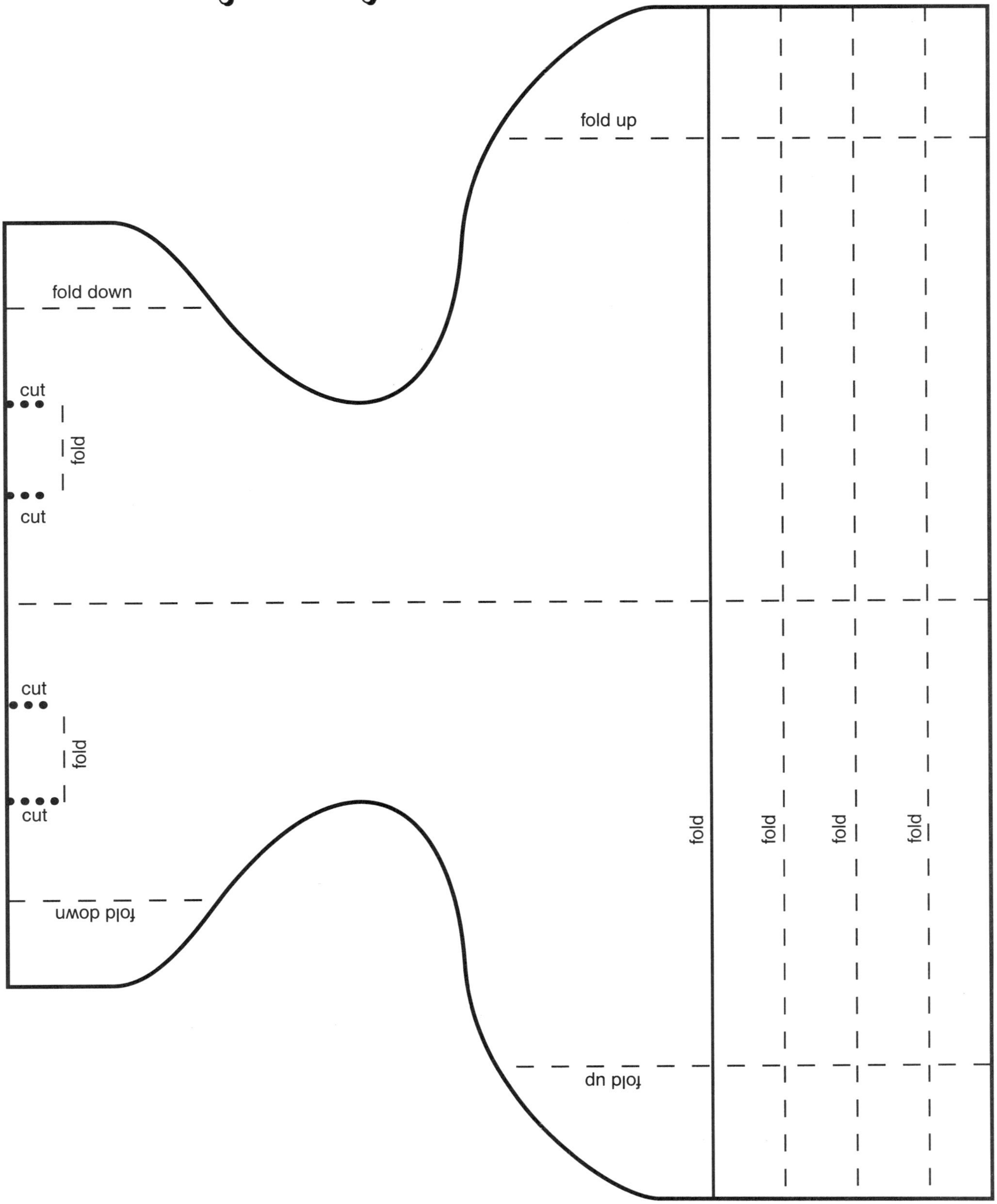
fold up
fold down
cut
fold
cut
cut
fold
cut
fold down
fold
fold
fold
fold
fold up

The T-Wing

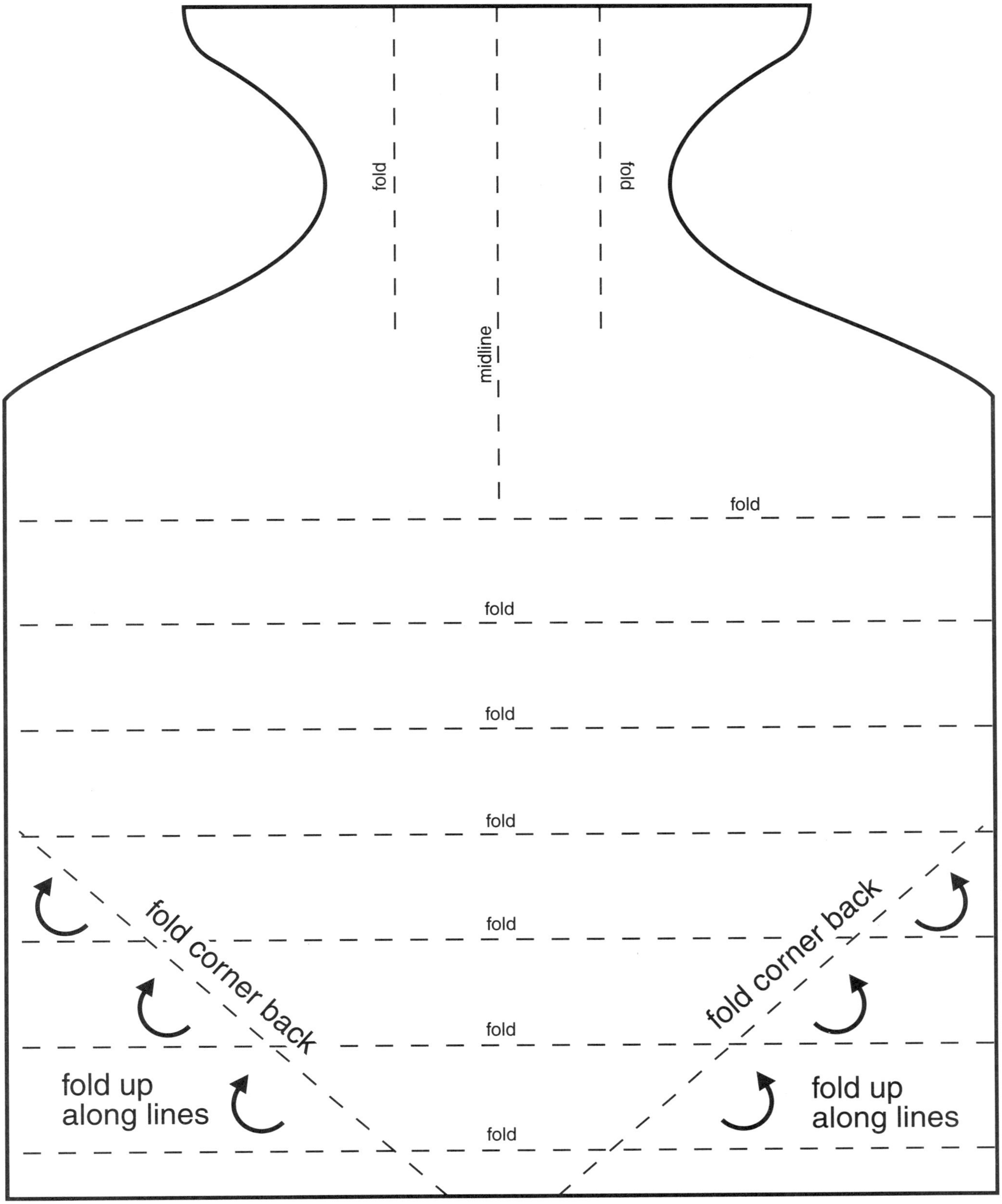
fold
midline
fold
fold
fold
fold
fold
fold
fold
fold
fold corner back
fold corner back
fold up
along lines
fold up
along lines

The Delta-1

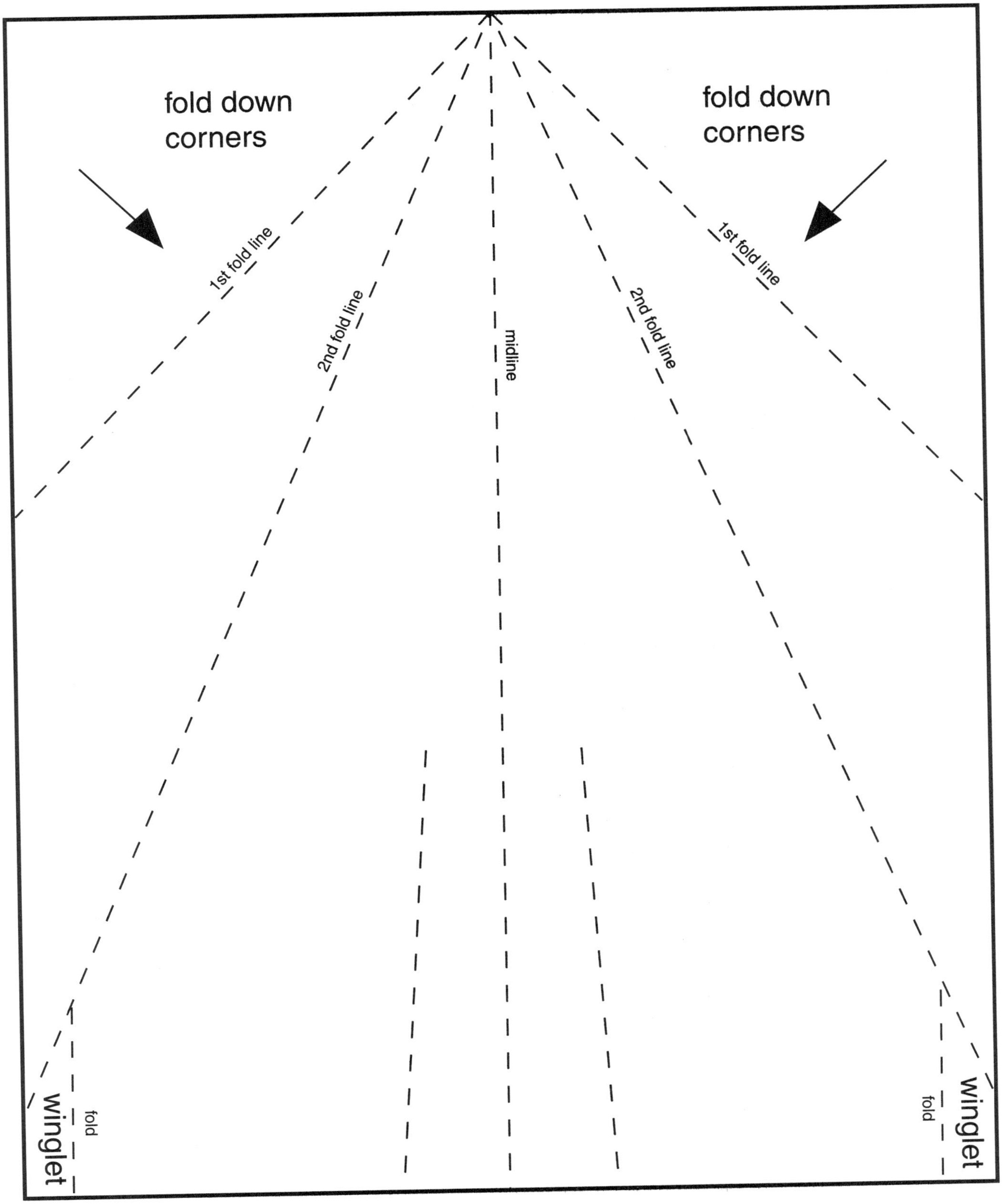
fold down corners
fold down corners
1st fold line
1st fold line
2nd fold line
2nd fold line
midline
winglet
fold
winglet
fold

The Straw de Loop

The Flying Napkin

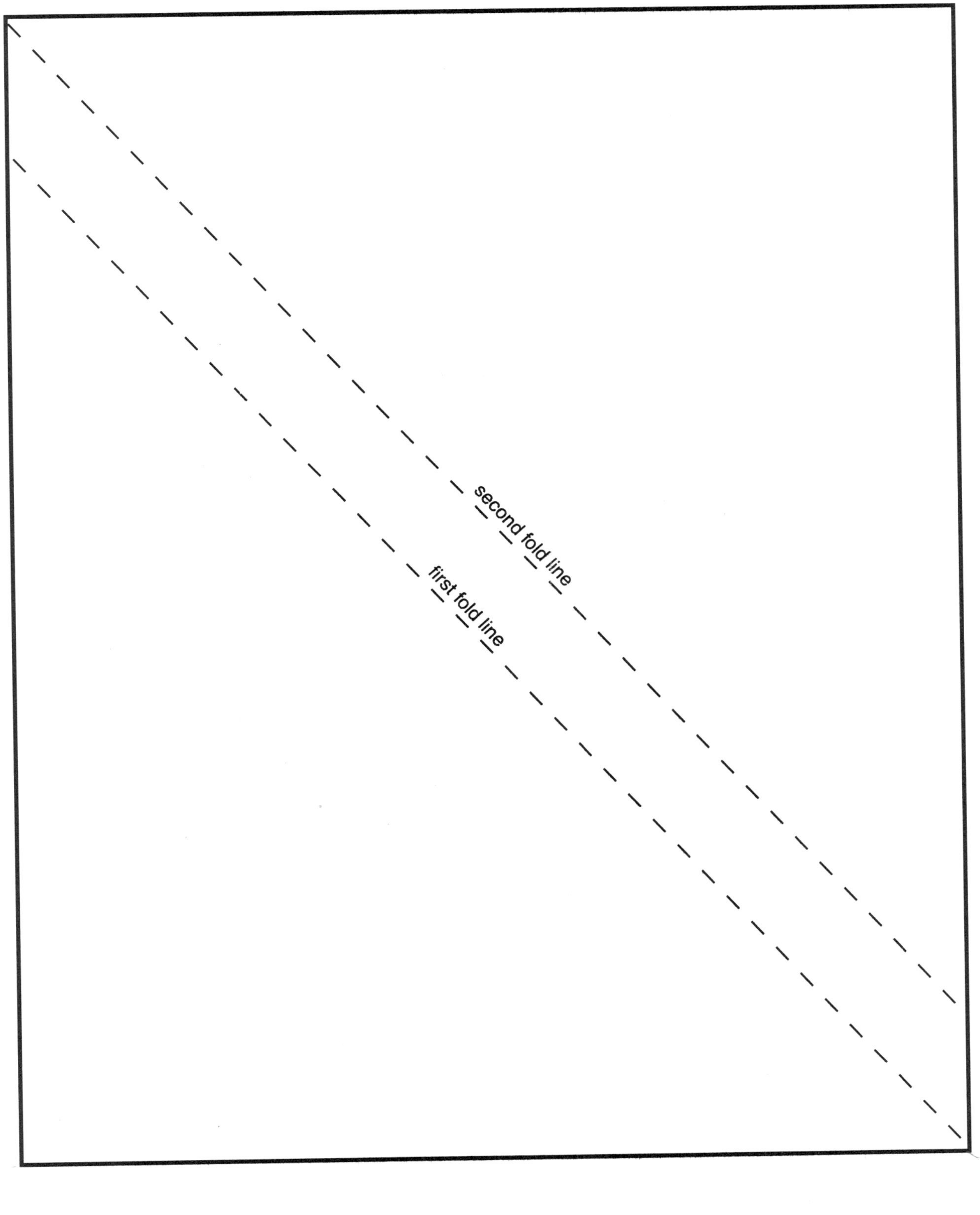

The Boomerang

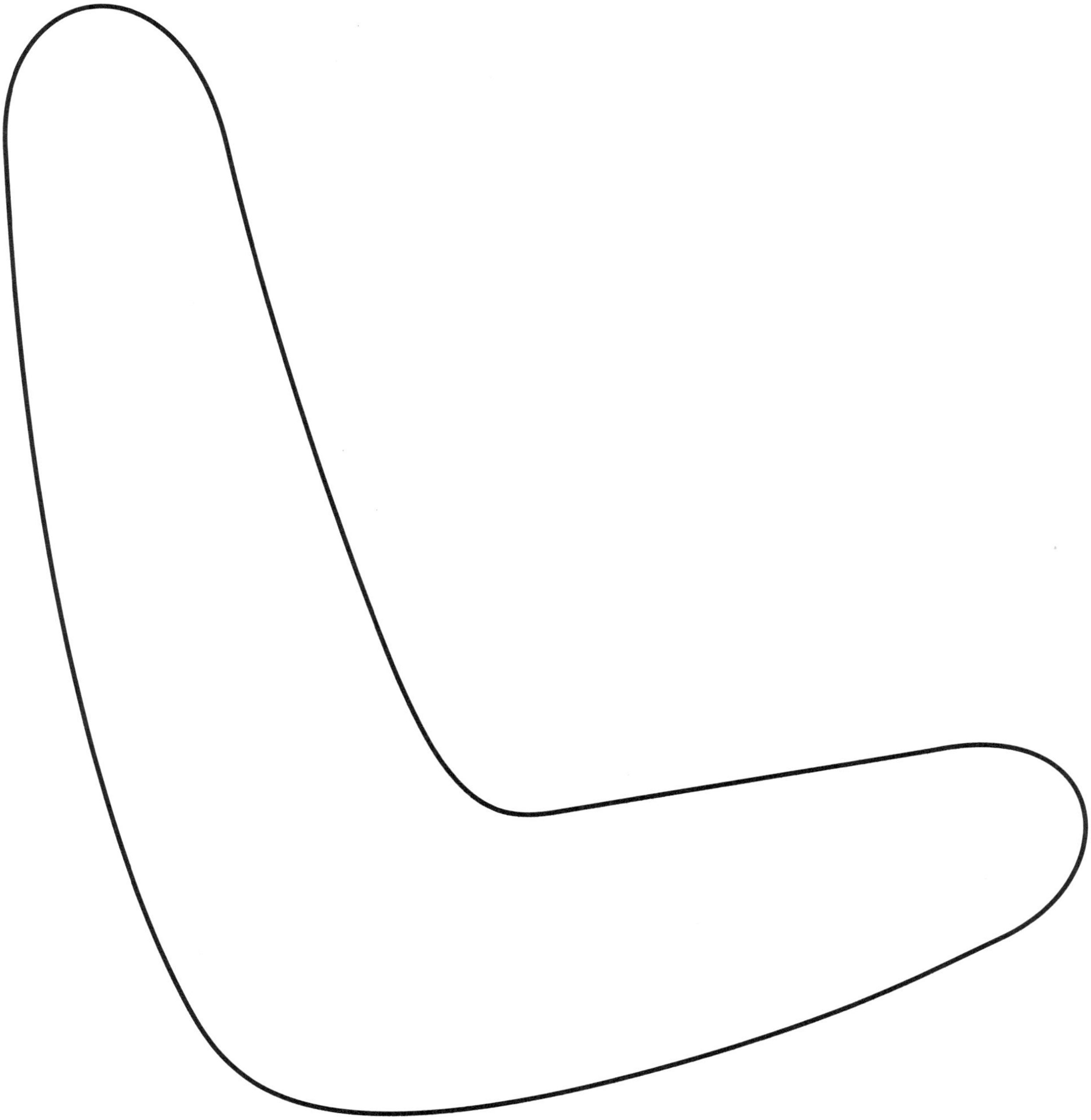

The Parachute

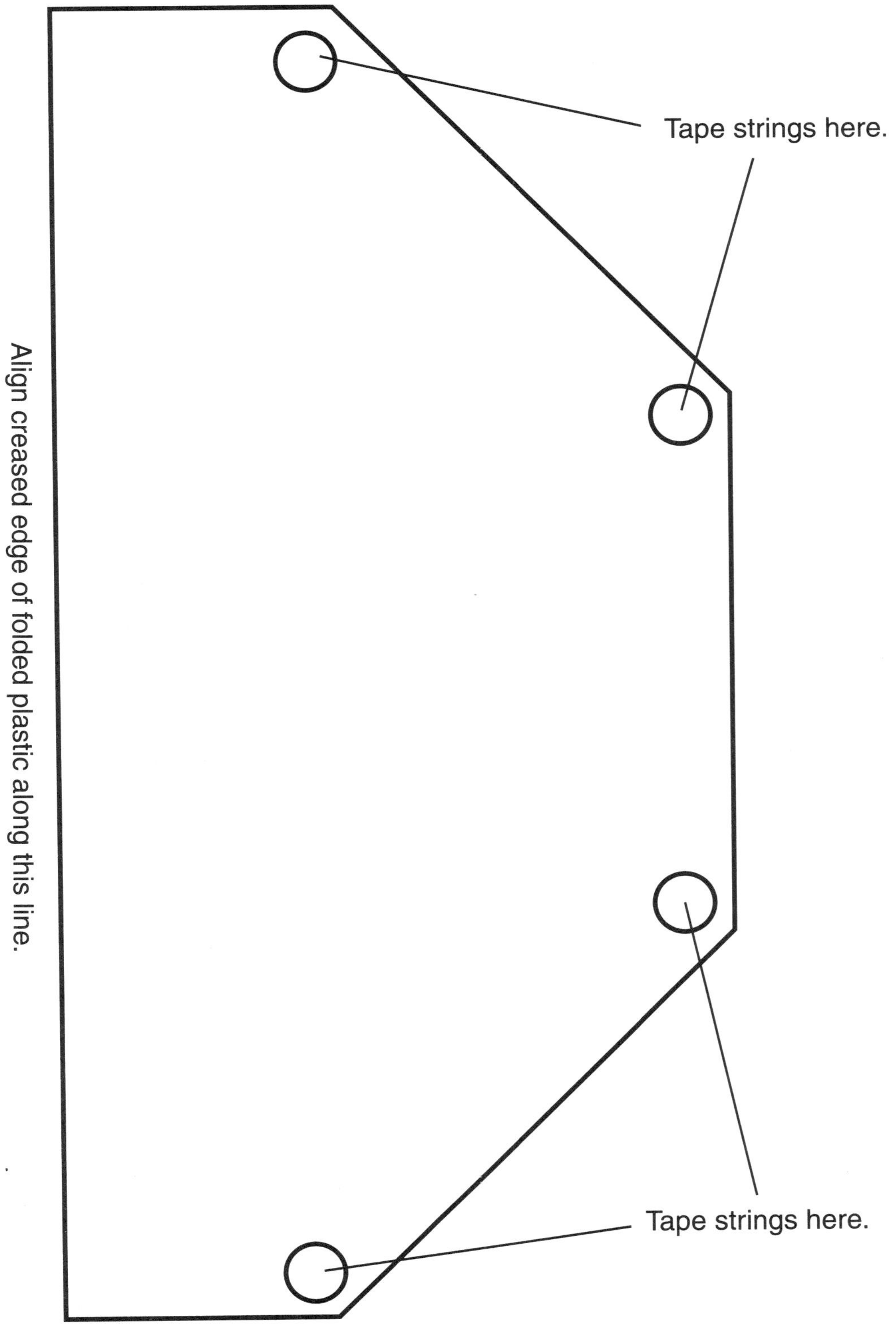

The Paraglide

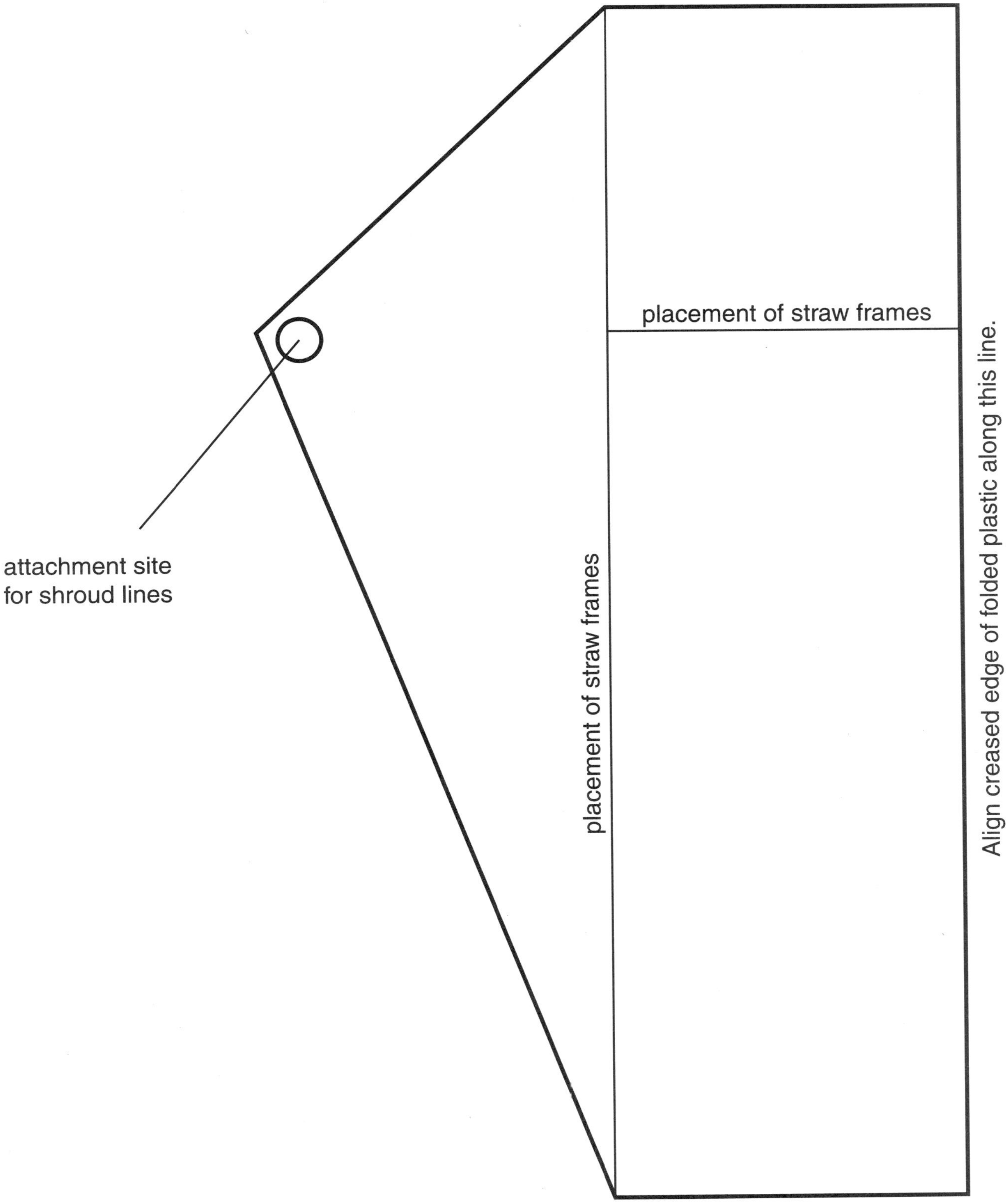

The Dragonfly

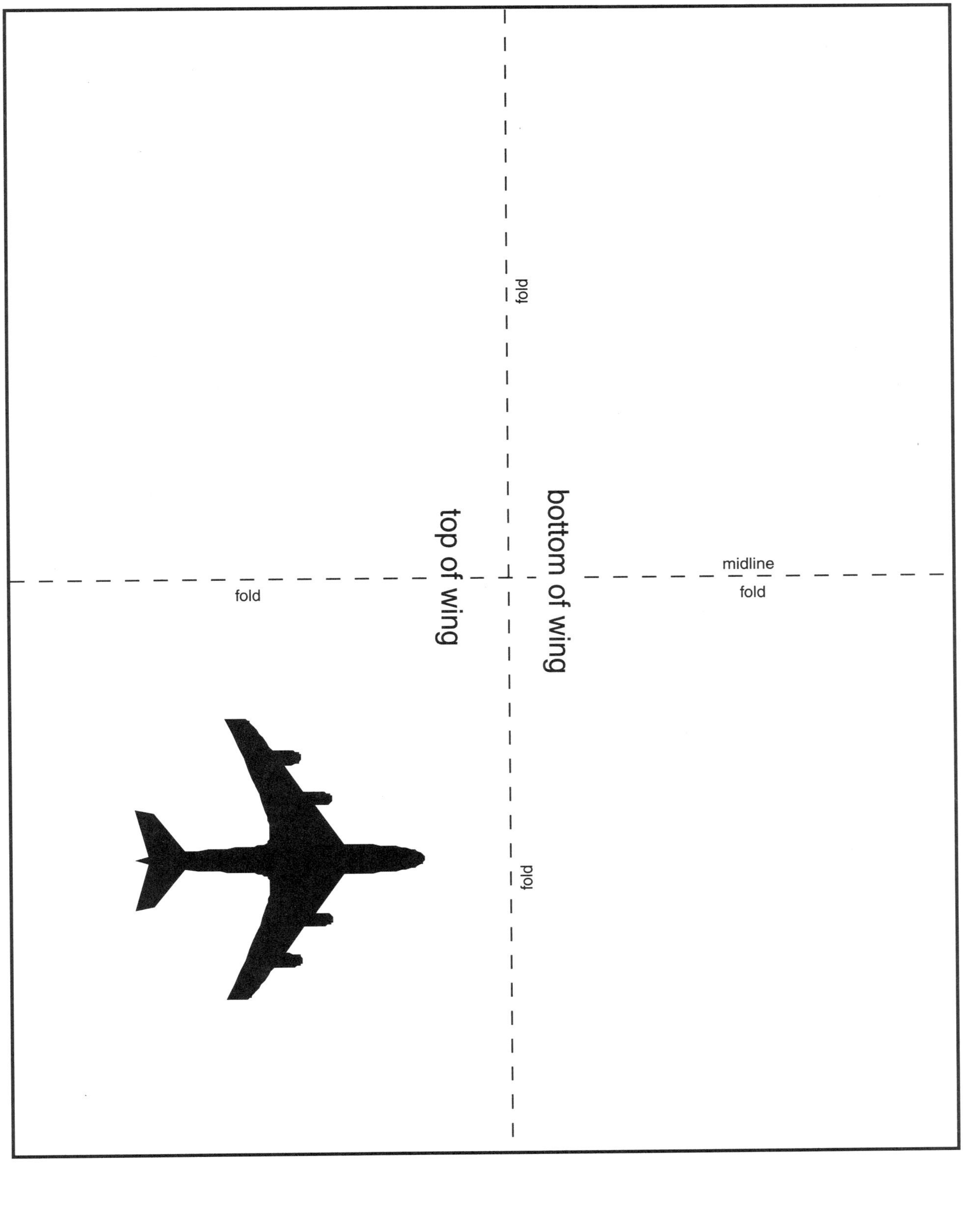